EUROPE & OUTREMER
(THE · HOLY · LAND)
Circa Anno Domini 1191

KINGDOM
OF
CYPRUS

Tyre

Acre

Jerusalem

MEDITERRANEAN SEA

DOMINIONS OF SALADIN

Map illustration © 2008 by Mike Reagan.

THE
YOUNGEST
TEMPLAR

BOOK THREE
ORPHAN OF DESTINY

THE YOUNGEST TEMPLAR

BOOK THREE
ORPHAN OF DESTINY

Michael P. Spradlin

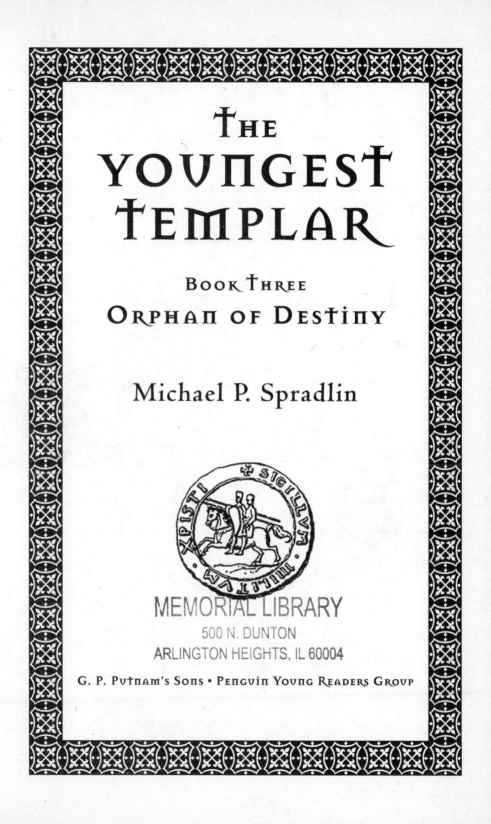

G. P. Putnam's Sons • Penguin Young Readers Group

G. P. PUTNAM'S SONS
A DIVISION OF PENGUIN YOUNG READERS GROUP.
Published by The Penguin Group.
Penguin Group (USA) Inc., 375 Hudson Street, New York, NY 10014, U.S.A.
Penguin Group (Canada), 90 Eglinton Avenue East, Suite 700, Toronto, Ontario M4P 2Y3, Canada
(a division of Pearson Penguin Canada Inc.).
Penguin Books Ltd, 80 Strand, London WC2R 0RL, England.
Penguin Ireland, 25 St. Stephen's Green, Dublin 2, Ireland (a division of Penguin Books Ltd.).
Penguin Group (Australia), 250 Camberwell Road, Camberwell, Victoria 3124, Australia
(a division of Pearson Australia Group Pty Ltd).
Penguin Books India Pvt Ltd, 11 Community Centre, Panchsheel Park, New Delhi - 110 017, India.
Penguin Group (NZ), 67 Apollo Drive, Rosedale, North Shore 0632, New Zealand
(a division of Pearson New Zealand Ltd).
Penguin Books (South Africa) (Pty) Ltd, 24 Sturdee Avenue, Rosebank, Johannesburg 2196, South Africa.
Penguin Books Ltd, Registered Offices: 80 Strand, London WC2R 0RL, England.
Copyright © 2010 by Michael P. Spradlin.
Map illustration © 2008 by Mike Reagan.

Printed in the United States of America.
Design by Marikka Tamura.
Text set in Centaur MT.
Library of Congress Cataloging-in-Publication Data
Orphan of destiny / Michael P. Spradlin ; [map illustration by Mike Reagan].
p. cm.—(The youngest Templar ; bk. 3)
Summary: Young Squire Tristan, Robard, Maryam and Angel make one last desperate push to deliver
the Holy Grail to safety in 1191 Scotland, but the way is full of danger as new enemies are met
and Sir Hugh attempts to thwart them at every turn.
[1. Knights and knighthood—Fiction. 2. Grail—Fiction. 3. Middle Ages—Fiction.
4. Europe—History—476–1492—Fiction.] I. Title.
PZ7.S7645Orp 2010 [Fic]—dc22 2010002856
ISBN 978-0-399-24765-1
1 3 5 7 9 10 8 6 4 2

This book is for the girls,
Pilar Elizabeth Mackey and Jordan Jean Mackey.
They are gifts to us all.

Don't miss

The
YOUNGEST
TEMPLAR

BOOK ONE
KEEPER OF THE GRAIL

BOOK TWO
TRAIL OF FATE

ACKNOWLEDGMENTS

If you are fortunate enough to be a published writer, you quickly learn that creating a finished book is a collaborative effort involving dozens of individuals. So I offer up sincere thanks to my agent, Steven Chudney, for patiently listening to my flood of ideas. To my editor, Tim Travaglini, for taking a jumbled mass of words and finding the story in it (I knew it was around here somewhere). To the incredible sales and marketing teams at Penguin Young Readers Group. To my colleagues Brian Murray, Josh Marwell, Michael Brennan, Carla Parker, Elise Howard and Liate Stehlik for their unflagging support. To Stephen Dafoe and Christine Leddon for their evangelical efforts on my behalf. To Shelly and Terry Palczewski for always showing up, even though they've heard it all before. Thanks to the staff at the Homer Public Library for a great event every year. To my mom and sisters for more support than I deserve. To my kids, Mick, Jessica and Rachel, for always letting me tell the stories. And to my wife, Kelly, for all of this and everything else. I couldn't love you more.

PROLOGUE

I am closer now, Sir Thomas.

Wherever you are, I believe you watch over me. And if such a thing is true, then you know how far I've come. Though I cannot claim it was all my doing. My friends Robard and Maryam have remained steadfast, and in their own way they have carried the Grail as well. I know you ordered me to tell not a soul, but I could no longer let them risk their lives without knowing why. And I found, in their friendship and fierce loyalty, a much lighter step along a very perilous path.

I am tired.

More tired than I have ever been. So weary my bones ache at the very thought of moving. When we stood in the Knights Hall, back in Acre, and you handed me this leather satchel, which never leaves my side, you gave me no indication of how far I would travel. Back to England, yes, but a much longer journey for my soul.

I have seen things, Sir Thomas.

Death and pain and love and joy. And more than once I have wanted to curse your name. To throw my arms to heaven and ask,

"Why me?" Who is this Tristan of St. Alban's that made a Knight of the Temple believe he was ever capable of so grave a duty?

I still carry your sword, sire.

And, I am ashamed to say, I will one day stand before my maker and tell him I have wielded it in anger. With it, I have taken the lives of other men. Those who wished to kill me, no doubt, but the truth of it brings me no peace.

I will carry on, my liege.

Like the monks who raised me, I cannot bear the thought of disappointing you. Your face haunts my dreams. You trained me well, sire. But many times I worry you did not train me well enough.

I know the power of the Grail, Sir Thomas.

In battle, or in danger, when all around me appears about to fall, I hear its song. Does it sound because I am righteous? Or does it seek to guide me down a path I am incapable of finding—too weak to find—on my own?

Where are you, Sir Thomas?

If you are watching over me, you see me standing on the edge of complete and utter failure. My friends may die, and their blood will be on my hands and seared into my heart. There is nothing left for me to do but fight on, as you told me. I will not quit. Nor will I stop until I have delivered the Grail as you commanded. Or I will die in the attempt.

I am tired.

But I will fight on, Sir Thomas.

I will fight on.

Calais, France
Early December 1191

I

 should have trusted Maryam. Friends, good friends, learn to believe in each other, especially when their lives are at stake. She was a member of Al Hashshashin, after all, and one of the smartest, most determined warriors I'd ever seen. In the past few months, she'd proven to be more than capable of saving herself. In attempting to rescue her, I would probably just be in her way.

Robard's arrow missed, of course. From his hiding place behind the wagon, in the bailey of the Queen Mother Eleanor of Aquitaine's castle, he rose and shot at the rope encircling Maryam's neck as she was about to be hanged by Sir Hugh. I held the Queen Mother at sword point, determined to take her life if need be. At least that's what I told myself. I was bluffing, of course. I would not kill the defenseless Eleanor. But in his madness to possess the Holy Grail, the most sacred relic in all of Christendom, Sir Hugh was determined to hang Maryam if I did not give it to him. He kicked at the barrel where she was perilously balanced. Except that Maryam was not quite ready to die yet.

The barrel teetered on its edge and Maryam wobbled, her legs bending to and fro, fighting for balance. As Robard's arrow buzzed through the air toward her impromptu gallows, the King's Guards shouted orders, but their voices drowned each other out.

Then, in my haste to reach Maryam, I roughly pushed Eleanor aside. It was a horrible mistake. Holding the Queen Mother hostage was our only advantage in a castle surrounded by heavily armed King's Guards and one decidedly insane Templar Knight, against just the three of us. Well, four of us, counting Angel.

"You'll die, boy," she sputtered at me on her way to the ground. "Mark my words, squire! I'll hunt you down and kill you myself before I ever let you threaten my son's rule!"

Sounds and noises were far off and distant in my head, and at that moment the Queen Mother's rant only blended into the chaos around me. Robard was screaming obscenities as Sir Hugh shouted at everyone to stay back, but I moved forward, sword at the ready.

It took only the briefest of moments for Robard's arrow to thunk into the wooden crossbeam where Maryam's rope was lashed. My heart sank. The dim torchlight revealed that he had missed. Not by much, but in this case even an inch meant death. I could not blame Robard. Aside from the flickering light, the night was pitch black. It was miraculous he had come so close. But it did not matter now. I would never forgive myself for her death, and as I ran toward her, I begged God to spare her soul.

But Maryam did not need saving. A split second before Sir Hugh's foot connected with the barrel, she launched herself into the air. I watched in amazement as she leapt high enough to grab the crossbeam with both hands. Sir Hugh looked up at her in confusion. He fully expected her to be dangling at the end of her rope, breathing her last. Instead, Maryam swung deftly upward until she was sitting on the crossbar of the windlass, which moments before had served as her gallows.

Sir Hugh cursed and swung his sword at her, and she pushed up on her hands to avoid the blade as it bit roughly into the wood. Another of Robard's arrows narrowly missed him, and he darted behind the wagon.

The Captain of the Guard moved to intercept me.

"Maryam! Catch!" I shouted, and tossed my short sword to her hilt first. She caught it easily and with one swing chopped through the rope and dropped to the ground. She now stood in Robard's line of fire, blocking his shot, as Sir Hugh stepped out to confront her. Al Hashshashin or not, Maryam could not match Sir Hugh's skill with the sword.

There was a squeal of pain as one of Robard's arrows found another guard.

The Captain was upon me. In our earlier encounters he had proven to be a most determined fellow. "Hold on, squire," he said, raising his sword. He expected that weaponless, I would be easily captured. But as he moved between me and Sir Hugh, I feinted to my left and he paused momentarily. With all the strength and momentum I could muster, I threw myself at his legs.

He tried to dodge out of the way, but I drove my shoulder into his waist. The air rushed out of his lungs, and with a grunt he was bent double and fell to the ground. As I landed on top of him, I drove my elbow into his chin and felt a satisfying crunch. His head flew back, hitting the cobblestone, and a low groan escaped his lips. His sword clattered away.

Not giving him a second to recover, I snatched up his weapon and scrambled to Maryam's side.

"Get to the horses! Robard is behind us! Hurry, before they close the gate!" I yelled to her.

Maryam leapt to the task. I stepped in front of her and Sir Hugh came at me with a vicious swing of his blade. The Captain's sword felt clumsy and unfamiliar in my hand, but I raised it quickly enough to block him, and sparks flew as our steel clashed.

"You'll die, squire," he spat at me. "Tonight, you will die." He swung again and I danced away, trying to put distance between us. Maryam quickly retrieved her daggers from the back of the wagon and slipped from sight. I had no desire to fight Sir Hugh. He was too strong and too experienced with the sword. I only needed to buy time.

"Tristan!" Robard yelled behind me. "Move! I can shoot him!"

Sir Hugh and I spun in unison. I dove to my right and he leapt behind the wagon again. Robard's arrow whistled through the air where Sir Hugh had stood just moments before. Was there no way to kill this man?

I glanced behind me. Two guards were shepherding the Queen Mother back into the keep, and the Captain still lay groaning on the ground. Three more guards hid behind a stone well that lay in the center of the bailey, pinned there by Robard and his bow.

We had to get out. I had no idea how many guards were on duty in the castle, but there must have been more than those assembled here. Richard the Lionheart would not leave such a small garrison protecting his mother. When word of this reached him, I knew I could add his name to a long list of enemies I was making.

I shot a glance at Sir Hugh again. He still hid behind the wagon, not eager to step out and risk Robard's wrath. In the flickering torchlight I could see the mask of fury on his face as his eyes darted back and forth between me and Robard.

"Tristan! Hurry!" Maryam shouted. She had found a few scattered horses in the confusion and was now mounted. She held the reins of two bay mares and steered them toward Robard's spot behind the wagon. He took a running start and leapt to the saddle, stilling the animal with his knees. Another arrow was nocked and ready in a heartbeat. Maryam waved my short sword at me. I didn't wait for Sir Hugh to act. I turned and sprinted the few yards between us and sprang up on the back of the empty horse.

"Angel! Here!" I yelled, and we turned and spurred hurriedly toward the castle entrance. She appeared out of the darkness, barking loudly.

Sir Hugh was raving, "The gate! Close the gate!" Someone in the tower must have heard him, for I could hear the loud clank of chains and watched in horror as it began its cumbersome descent.

Maryam and Robard had nearly reached the exit, but just as they were about to ride through, two King's Guards rushed them from each side of the closing gate, swords drawn.

I thought they would try to take out the horses, but Robard shot first, hitting one in the leg with an arrow. The man cried out, falling to the ground, and Robard's mount nearly trampled him as he rode by. But the altercation spooked Maryam's horse and it reared. I steered to the right of her, determined to protect her from the second guard.

Maryam fought the horse, which was now in a full rage, bucking and snorting. Angel and Robard had made it through the gate

7

and waited outside. Robard pulled another arrow but was unsure what to do.

Maryam tried her best, but the horse would not settle. Finally she let go of the reins and jumped from its back. It skittered away, blowing and kicking.

Out of the confusion Sir Hugh charged from behind the wagon, sword raised.

"Tristan! Maryam! Get out of there!" Robard shouted.

The three King's Guards hiding behind the well also took up the chase. The one by the door advanced on Maryam, whose back was momentarily to him. He held Sir Thomas' battle sword.

"Maryam! Watch out!" I yelled in warning.

Maryam acted instantaneously, turning and drawing her weapons in one motion. The guard was upon her, and he swung the sword down with all his might. She crossed her daggers over her head, catching the blade and twisting the sword from his grip as I had seen her do so many times. For good measure, she kicked the man hard in the groin, and with an agonizing squeal he fell to the ground.

The gate continued toward the ground.

"Maryam, the sword!" I hollered. She scooped up Sir Thomas' battle sword and ran through the gate. I spurred my horse right after her and had just enough room to duck beneath the gate.

"Let's go!" said Robard. He held out his hand to Maryam, who pulled herself up onto the horse behind him.

"Wait!" I cried, sliding from the back of my horse. "Robard, give me cover!"

"What are you . . . ?" But he turned his horse and, standing in the stirrups, shot through the gate at the legs of someone chasing us. The arrow missed and stuck in the ground, but I heard shrieks of alarm.

Sir Hugh's high-pitched, venomous voice commanded someone to raise the gate, but in the confusion it kept sliding downward.

"Tristan! What are you doing?" Maryam yelled at me.

The gate was made of thick oak planks. Two large beams on each side formed a groove that held it in place as it was raised and lowered. Quickly, I took the Captain's sword and jammed the point into the groove between the door and the beam. I pulled back on the hilt with all my might and, digging my heels into the ground, snapped six inches of the steel blade off at the tip. I jammed the remaining length in the gap again, right next to the first piece. It was much more difficult to work into the groove a second time, but finally, after pushing it in as hard as I could, it held fast. I hoped it would stop the door from being raised from the inside and give us time to put distance between us and the pursuit sure to follow.

"Good idea!" said Robard. Maryam laughed.

"What are you laughing at?" I asked as I mounted my horse.

"You. How did you think to jam the door?" she asked.

"I planned it all along," I said confidently. "Once we got out, of course."

"You planned it," she said in disbelief.

"Certainly."

"Sure you did," she replied.

There was no time to answer. With Angel in tow, we rode off into the night.

Sir Hugh was long from finished with us.

2

 well-traveled road led directly from the castle into Calais.

"Where to, squire?" Robard asked. His voice was strong and deep over the rushing wind and clatter of hooves. In the moonlight, Maryam clutched him tightly around the waist, her face buried in his shoulder. His relief at having her back and unhurt was evident in his tone and manner.

"Head for the docks. We need to acquire a ship or boat and cross the channel as quickly as we can," I answered.

"Acquire?" Maryam queried, a teasing tone in her voice.

"I do not welcome another sea voyage, but we cannot walk to England. My trick with the Captain's sword will not stay the castle door for long." I dug my heels into the horse's flank and pulled ahead of my friends. Angel ran before us, leading the way.

Robard and Maryam loved to make sport of my plans. It was their own fault, since they left all the thinking to me. Still, it was hard to blame them for being concerned. I had managed to get us into a number of dangerous situations. Yet, here we were, free again, at least temporarily.

Sir Hugh wasted little time. As the castle receded behind us, the sound of a loud horn cut through the darkness. We reined up and saw men atop the battlements waving torches back and forth. From the town below us, a bell sounded a few moments later and the shouts of men carried on the wind.

"What's happening?" Maryam asked.

"I don't know. Sir Hugh has sounded the alarm. The castle must have a way of alerting the village. If there are soldiers or Templars quartered there, we must be doubly careful!" We galloped away, and I feared our pursuers were close at hand. Had they managed to raise the gate?

Within minutes we reached the outskirts of Calais. There were few villagers about at this hour, and only the faintest trace of starlight guided our way.

"Which way?" Robard asked.

"Robard," I said, exasperated, "we need a boat. I believe boats are kept at or near the ocean."

"Don't get testy with me, squire," Robard muttered. I felt bad momentarily, but I was trying to think. Something was telling me to avoid the village.

"Hold," I said, pulling the reins as my horse skidded to a stop. We had entered on a deserted street, lined by a few simple huts. A pathway between the structures led farther into the heart of the town.

"What's wrong?" Maryam asked.

"I did not count on Sir Hugh being able to sound a warning. No one here will know exactly what to look for, but they know the castle has raised an alarm. I'm wondering if—" My words were cut off by a whizzing sound, and I cried out as a crossbow bolt thunked into the pommel of my saddle. My horse jumped and bolted forward, and I nearly lost my grip.

"Go!" Robard yelled. He slapped reins and we darted forward, our horses churning up ground as the small huts flew by. Off to our right I could hear shouts of "After them!" and "This way!" I had no idea yet if our pursuers were mounted or on foot, but they were most definitely armed. I understood Robard's disdain of the crossbow. The distinctive twang of a bowstring and the flight of an arrow from a longbow made noise as it traveled through the air. At least it gave one a fighting chance to dodge or drop to the ground to avoid it. You never heard a crossbow bolt until it appeared, as if by magic, in the center of your chest.

"Stay low," Robard shouted, bending forward, hugging his mount's neck. I did the same and could swear I felt the air move as another bolt hummed by where my head had been moments before.

The hard ground turned to cobblestone as we entered Calais proper, and the clatter of hoofbeats thundered through the darkness. Soon, buildings lined both sides of the street and the noise of our escape echoed off the walls. Up ahead, I thought I saw movement and warned Robard to turn.

"LEFT, Robard! LEFT!" I shouted. He steered as I commanded down a side street. We were not getting closer to the docks by this route, and finding a boat seemed unlikely. Our abrupt turn gained us some distance on those following us, but it sounded as if several squads of men were moving through the town in an effort to surround us. I believed we were riding south, which would put us parallel to the coast, but I couldn't be sure. The streets were narrow and dark, and it was easy to get turned around.

We had nearly reached the southern edge of Calais, and through a break in the buildings I could see the ocean, and regained my bearings.

"Tristan?" Robard said.

"This way!" I gave rein and pulled ahead of him. Angel was barking madly in the dark, and the village dogs took up the chorus. We were making more noise than a regimento of Templars in full-scale battle. I turned my horse toward the ocean. Somewhere ahead, there must be a boat for us.

We darted and weaved through the streets and alleys. I could hear more horses and knew the longer we waited, the better the chances that Sir Hugh would arrive from the castle with even more men. I cursed my stupidity for heading straight to the village. We should have ridden north or south and found a boat along the coast somewhere. My eagerness to get away from him had clouded my judgment.

The moon peeked over the horizon to the northwest. It was late in the year, so it would stay low in the sky, but the extra light was a blessing and a curse.

"Hold," I said, and we pulled our horses to a stop.

"Why are we stopping?" Maryam asked.

"We need to get off these streets," I said. "With the moon rising we'll be seen, so we need to be quiet." I nudged my horse forward at a walk. "We need to head for the countryside. Find a place where we—"

"No," Robard said quietly.

"What?" I replied.

"I said no. We're getting a boat and getting out of this bloody country," he declared.

"Robard, that is not a good idea," I explained. "The alarm has been raised; they will be waiting at the docks—"

"Then I'll shoot them," he interrupted, shaking his bow at me.

"Robard, maybe Tristan is right—" Maryam said.

"Not tonight." Robard pointed over his shoulder toward the ocean. "England lies across that water. Home is so close I can almost smell it. I'll not wait another night. Not another minute. I will kill every King's Guard with my bare hands if I have to. But we sail tonight."

The moonlight played across Robard's face. It had turned to stone, and I could see it would be useless to argue.

My shoulders sagged as exhaustion hit me. I was so tired. My head still ached from being knocked unconscious when we had first been captured. I couldn't think. Angel growled from a few paces away, her nose working the air, and her head turned to look off toward the way we had come.

"Someone is coming," Maryam said.

"All right. Let's skirt the town; avoid the cobblestone streets where possible. We'll make less noise. We'll circle around to the docks. Perhaps they are not guarded yet," I said. But my words held little enthusiasm.

"Excellent," Robard said.

A few minutes of careful riding later, we rode back into the town, with the channel to our left. We stopped, momentarily, listening. It was strangely quiet. Perhaps we had temporarily eluded those chasing us. Could we have been lucky enough for them to lose our trail? Did they assume we had ridden away to the countryside?

"I don't hear anything. Do you?" Robard asked.

"Yes. I hear a voice. Telling me over and over that this is a very bad idea."

Robard snorted in reply. His mind was made up.

We walked the horses a few hundred yards farther into town, and up ahead I could see a single wooden wharf extending out into the harbor, with several small boats tied to it. Farther out, larger vessels bobbed gently at anchor. The waterfront was lined by a row of shops, inns and other buildings. They all were dark this time of night and their emptiness felt wrong. It was too quiet.

"Let's go the rest of the way on foot," I suggested. "We can tie the horses here, and if it's a trap, we may be able to recover them."

Robard did not disagree. We tied both of them to a nearby post and made our way toward freedom, keeping to the shadows as much as possible.

"Angel, lead," I said. As always, the little golden dog appeared to know exactly what I needed. She trotted about twenty paces ahead of us, cocking her head left and right, pausing occasionally and sniffing at the ground.

Robard held his bow at the ready, Maryam had drawn her daggers and my short sword rested comfortably in my hand. I could barely breathe as we crept forward, my eyes scanning every nook and cranny, any spot where a man with a crossbow might conceal himself.

I saw nothing.

We waited, keeping the dock in sight, hoping anyone hiding there might grow careless and reveal their presence.

"All clear," said Robard.

He stepped out of the shadows and crossed the street, the dock only a few paces away. Maryam followed closely, and then it was my turn.

As I ventured into the street, I felt something punch me in my right side. Worse than a punch—a punch would not hurt as much. I looked down at my right hip and was shocked to see a crossbow bolt protruding from it. The pain was instantaneous and immense.

"Beauseant!" I shouted, not knowing why I chose to utter the Templar battle cry. I tried to step forward, to warn Robard and Maryam, but my leg was not working correctly. Angel barked and I heard Maryam's ululating war cry and Robard's curse. His bow twanged and someone screamed. Then another cry and the sound of running feet. My vision swirled and I thought for a moment I was back in Acre, with Sir Thomas beside me.

"Sir Thomas commands . . ." I could not finish, for it hurt even to breathe. I saw Maryam's flashing daggers and heard a groan of anguish, and I believe someone died right in front of me.

Then I heard a familiar soft humming sound, coming from everywhere and nowhere all at once. I felt warm and strangely comforted by it. Nearby came the sounds of running feet and shouts of angry men. And as the ground rushed up to meet me, my last thought was, Please don't let me die in France.

Somewhere in the English Channel

3

 felt the sensation of movement, rising and falling. And I smelled and tasted salt. It made me sick to my stomach, and I thought I would vomit.

The next time I woke up, I could feel the wind blowing in my face. But we weren't moving as much as before.

My eyes opened to a blue sky. Then they closed, and when they opened again, the night sky and stars were above me. They shut once more, and I could no longer see stars, but light came from somewhere. I thought I heard Robard say, "He's awake." But I drifted off again before I could answer him.

When I next came to, I was standing in a gently rolling grassy field. There was a soft breeze, and the sun, high in the cloudless sky, was warm on my face. A shadow fell across me, and I glanced up to see a bird, a very large bird, circling lazily in the sky. It flew up until it almost disappeared from sight, and then it flexed its wings and dove. It picked up speed and I watched, transfixed, as it headed straight for me. I smiled in wonder at the grace of what

I first thought was a kestrel of some sort, but as it drew closer, it grew in size and kept growing, and I worried it might be some larger bird that would sink its talons into me.

I turned and ran, and the shadow of the bird covered the sun and the light dimmed. Then came a horrible shriek, high-pitched and cackling, and the bird began laughing. Impossible, I told myself. Birds don't laugh.

My boots grew heavy and I looked down at my wound to see that blood was seeping through the bright white tunic I wore. It had a brilliantly colored red cross embroidered on the chest. The shadow was almost upon me, and as I stole a glance over my shoulder, I screamed out loud, for it was no bird at all. It was a large and powerful dragon, and its face was the face of Eleanor, the Queen Mother. As the giant talons of the beast reached out for me, I clutched at my belt for my sword but was dismayed to find myself unarmed. I tripped and fell to the ground, tumbling hard, crying in agony at the pain in my side.

The next thing I knew, I lay flat on the ground, and Eleanor of Aquitaine stood with one tiny foot on my chest as if she had just bested me in a wrestling match. Perhaps she had, for my head felt thick and dull, and I could not raise my arms. She peered down at me, and her face became curiously hawklike and her eyes blackened. I wished to close my eyes but could not.

"Look at this, poor little orphan boy. You've been shot, orphan boy! What idiot walks right into an ambush? And you think you could be a king?" With that she threw back her head, and her cackling laugh rang through the air around me.

"What?" I managed to say. Her head snapped down, and her eyes bore into me. "Me, a king? I'm not . . . I do not . . . I have no idea what you're talking about!" And truer words were never spoken. I remembered her admonition as I'd held her hostage in the castle. "I'll see you dead before you ever sit on Richard's throne," she had sputtered at me. I'd paid little attention to her at the time. It made no sense to me.

"And I'm supposed to believe that!" She pressed her foot directly onto my wound, and I moaned in agony.

"No!" I shouted back at her. "Stop! I don't know what you're talking about!"

"Ha!" she said to me. "You think me so foolish? Thomas Leux served my husband! Always there to lick Henry's boots! He told you! I know he did! Don't lie to me, *orphan boy!*"

She literally spat the words at me. In all my life, with everything I'd seen, even on the battlefield, I don't think I'd ever come across someone so angry and full of hate. She pushed her foot against my wound again, and the pain caused me to cry out, "I AM NOT A KING!"

Water splashed into my face and the Queen disappeared, replaced by Maryam, who stood over me, holding a dripping water skin.

"Easy, Templar," she said. "We know you are most definitely not a king." I tried to explain how the Queen Mother was tormenting me, but I was too weak and the words would not come. I closed my eyes.

When I next woke, water was being poured over my lips. It tasted wonderful. Something licked my face, and I hoped it was Angel, but in my disoriented state I couldn't be sure it wasn't the Queen Mother or, knowing my luck, a large Eleanor-shaped dragon.

My dreams took me to the walls above Acre over the main city gate. Sir Thomas stood next to me, resplendent in his bright white tunic and gleaming chain mail. His battle sword hung at his side, his hand gripping the hilt. His reddish brown hair blew about his head in the breeze. Sir Basil, with his loyal squire Quincy, stood not far away. They both beamed at me. The lilting tenor of the Grail carried through the air around us, but strangely they did not notice it.

Sir Thomas studied the field below Acre, his face a mask of seriousness. When I tried to see, to understand what drew his attention, I could not. The field appeared deserted to me, but I also heard the sounds of an invisible battle played out before us. My confusion exhausted me.

Sir Thomas put his hand on my shoulder. "Are you ready, lad?" he asked me.

"Ready for what, Sir Thomas?" I replied.

"It's almost here," he said.

"What, Sir Thomas?" I asked. "What is almost here? Why are you here? I left you behind. Am I to rejoin you? . . . Am . . . am I dying?"

"No, lad. You are almost finished with your duty. But you must not come here. Not yet. Your task is not complete, and danger lies this way. You must be more careful than ever. You cannot lose. We cannot lose. Return and finish what you've begun. You've been so brave. I told you in Acre, Sir Lancelot himself had no finer squire. Remember?"

"Yes, sire," I said. "I remember." The warmth of his words brought me happiness for a moment.

"It's true. Now go. Finish this. You can do it. We did not choose you for this duty—the Grail did. Remember it sounds only for the righteous. Go, lad. You will not face this danger alone, I promise. But still, be careful."

"Sir Thomas." I bowed my head. "I broke my vow. You ordered me to tell no one I carried the Grail. Not even a brother Templar. But Maryam and Robard deserved to know. And Celia. Sir Hugh was . . . I had to . . ." In my dream, it was difficult to talk and explain myself.

Sir Thomas gazed off to the plains below us for several long seconds. I feared he was angry, but he smiled. "Worry not, lad. You've chosen your friends well. I could have done no better. You've more than served your oath to me, Tristan. But you must finish it." His voice was firm and filled with determination. "Do not forget, help will be there when you need it."

The musical sound of the Grail grew louder, and it was impossible for me to understand how Sir Thomas could not hear it. It was louder than it had ever been before. Yet Sir Thomas just smiled and nodded at me.

Then he faded away, as did Quincy and Sir Basil. But I remained standing on the high wall above Acre, the sun shining brightly and a breeze caressing my face. I was happy. Happier than I'd ever been. With a smile, I glanced backward, studying the walls and rooftops of the city below me. Slowly, I realized that it was deserted and I was alone. If I stayed there, I would be companionless forever. Was this why Sir Thomas told me I didn't belong here? Was he worried I would spend eternity in solitude?

When I next woke, I heard songbirds, and waves crashing against the shore. I was lying on the ground but remembered being on a boat at some point. How long had I been out? I tried to rise, but a hand pushed my head gently back down. A voice told me to rest, and though I wished to disobey, I could not. More sleep.

Finally I was conscious, but it was dark. I heard Maryam and Robard talking quietly. I tried to speak, but no words would come, and there was a burning, throbbing, stinging pain in my side. It was as if there was a hornet's nest beneath the hide and muscle of my hip. Then I remembered the fight at the docks in Calais, and a crossbow bolt protruding from my side.

Something warm, rough and damp touched my cheek, and the smell of wet dog assaulted my nose. There was another odor, a fire burning, the smell of something cooking. The sense of all these things surrounded me, and I pushed and concentrated and lunged up from the depths of unconsciousness. My eyes flew open and I gasped aloud, "Hornets!"

Light reflected off a large boulder where I lay sprawled on the ground, and in an instant the faces of Angel, Maryam and Robard appeared above me.

"He's finally awake," Robard said.

"Tristan, how are you feeling?" Maryam asked.

Angel barked.

"I feel . . . Where did . . . pain?"

"Where did the pain come from?" Maryam tried to finish my sentence for me. "You were shot. By a crossbow. You lost a lot of blood. We thought we were going to lose you more than once." Her hand tenderly pushed the hair from my eyes.

"What happened?" I asked.

"What do you remember?" Robard asked back.

"We were on the street, close to the docks. Then something

24

punched me in the side and I looked down to see a bolt. Not much after that. The King's Guards showed up, didn't they?" The pain in my hip rose up and nausea overtook me. Closing my eyes and breathing deeply, I tried to settle myself.

"He should rest," Maryam said. "It makes no difference what happened. We're safe for now."

I opened my eyes again and saw something pass between Robard and Maryam. He stalked away from the fire out of my line of sight. I tried to follow him with my eyes but couldn't yet.

"What's wrong?" I asked her quietly.

She pushed a log deeper into the fire. "He blames himself for your getting shot. He insisted we sail immediately, and now he feels foolish and selfish. I've told him you would never blame him, but he's a hard one. Hardest on himself, actually. He—"

"I'm standing right here. I can hear you!" Robard exclaimed from somewhere behind me.

Finally I was able to rise up on my elbows and scoot around to sit leaning against the boulder. Angel scurried next to me and curled herself up next to my hip and went immediately to sleep. How often I envied dogs.

"Robard, don't fret about it. We were surrounded, with pursuers all over the town. Trouble would have found us no matter where we went."

He relaxed his stance a bit. We had traveled together long enough for me to know he would condemn himself for a long time over my wound.

"It's my fault, squire," he said. "If I weren't so headstrong on the idea of getting home—"

"Robard, had you not insisted on heading straight to the docks,

I would have worried something was wrong with you. Since I met you in Outremer, you've spoken of little else but returning to your forest. It was wrong of me to think otherwise. It's done. I'm going to be fine, so let us speak no more of it." He looked at me and smiled. His hair now reached his big shoulders, and his fair skin was windburned. But his blue eyes were clear and strong. When I was growing up at St. Alban's, Brother Rupert often told me tales of the Viking hordes who swept over England many hundreds of years ago. I had no doubt Robard was their heir. He finally relaxed a little more, then rested with his bow on the ground and his arms crossed over it.

"You gave us a fright," he said. Maryam concurred.

"You were delirious and running a horrible fever. Ranting out of your head," she said. "For a while, I didn't think we'd ever make the shore. But we finally landed not too far from here."

"Where is here? Where are we?" I asked.

Robard smiled. "We're home, Tristan. We're in England."

obard and Maryam recounted the events of the last two days. My memory ended at the docks, with the crossbow bolt sticking out of my hip.

"There were four of them waiting there," Maryam said. "Sir Hugh will be furious they let us slip away. Robard wounded two of them. My daggers claimed another. The other one turned and ran."

"We gathered you up," Robard went on, "and found a suitable vessel, small, much like the one in Tyre, only less of a wreck. It had three oars to a side, and we cut it loose and I started rowing while Maryam tried to keep you from bleeding the boat full and sinking us on the spot."

I winced at the thought.

"So much blood for a tiny flesh wound," Maryam remarked.

"Tiny?" I said, agitated.

Maryam shrugged. "It wasn't like you were shot by a longbow."

I glared at her. Maryam's compassion apparently had its limits.

"Didn't they try to chase us?" I asked.

"Of course," Maryam said. "They took two boats out right away, but I rowed and Robard discouraged them from getting too close. When we cleared the harbor and he had wounded a third man, they turned back. While you were sleeping, Robard and I kept going until we could no longer lift our arms.

"When we had a moment where it appeared no one was pursuing us, we removed the bolt. You were lucky. The guard was either a poor shot or he only sought to wound you. It was buried deep in the flesh of your hip and you lost a lot of blood. But it was not a killing blow. Robard held you down while I removed it." She added, "It was not pleasant."

"She means you screamed like a little gi—like a person in great pain," Robard corrected himself as he felt the sting of Maryam's baleful stare. "Grew up in a monastery, you say? Never heard such curse words."

My face grew hot with embarrassment.

"Stop teasing him, Robard," Maryam insisted. "You're lucky *you've* never felt an arrow pierce your thick hide. I can assure you it hurts, although a longbow does hurt more."

"Thank you, Maryam. . . . Robard, I don't know what I would have done if you hadn't stopped those Guards from capturing us," I said.

"Most likely died," Robard replied. Maryam and I both couldn't help but laugh. We were all relieved to at least be temporarily free and alive.

"So you rowed us all the way to England?" I asked.

Robard and Maryam looked at each other, something passed between them and they decided to abruptly change the subject.

"Yes, well, now we've arrived in England and I've found it cold, gray and wet. Why didn't the two of you tell me the sun never shines here?" she said.

"It does," we both answered at once.

"Well, we've been here three days and all it has done is rain and grow colder by the minute," she complained. She pulled her tunic up around her neck and scooted closer to the fire.

"Go back to the how-you-sailed-here part," I said. "I'm not quite following."

"I need to go on a scout," Robard said, "and see if I can find a stand of birch where there might be some seedlings. I have a few points left and need to make some arrows." He fussed with his wallet, counting the shafts he had left.

"All right, both of you stop. Tell me what happened," I insisted.

Robard swallowed. Maryam was silent. Apparently it was his tale to tell.

"Nothing happened. Not really. It wasn't a very large vessel. Three oars and a small sail.

"We tied you down in the front and rowed until we were well out into the channel. After the other boats turned back, we kept at it. You were still bleeding and crying out all the time. After a while we got tired and I thought it might be better if we raised the sail and caught the wind. We just pointed it west and hoped for the best," Robard said.

"You hoped for the best?" I asked, incredulous.

"Yes," he replied, suddenly interested in the maintenance of his bow.

I stared at both of them.

"What?" they both asked.

"That was your plan? Every time I come up with an idea, you two do nothing but belittle it. But when I'm lying near death, you put me in a boat and 'point it west' and 'hope for the best'?" The very thought of it made my wound throb again. "My goodness! What if the wind and current carried you past England? What if you were pushed back to France? Do you even know how to *sail*?"

"Of course—we sailed all the time in Sherwood Forest," Robard answered sarcastically. "What are you worried about? We got here, didn't we? Sailing isn't as hard as it seems, as long as there's wind. Without the wind, there's all the rowing, and that's some work, I'll tell you. Luckily, though, being an archer is ideally suited for rowing, as we tend to be strong in the arms. So I was able to compensate for Maryam . . . I mean when Maryam tired. . . ." Too late, Robard, my friend.

"Robard," Maryam said quietly. "I don't think we really want to talk about this *now*, do we?"

"Um. No. I guess not," he replied sheepishly.

"Anyhow, it worked, didn't it? Here we are, safe in England," Robard said.

"Ohh," I said. I had to lie back against the rock and close my eyes. Weakness washed over me, and I covered my face with my hands. "And the two of you have the gall to complain . . . I'm the one without plans . . . ," I muttered. "Where in England?" I asked, sitting up again.

"What did he say?" Robard asked.

"Nothing," Maryam said. "Tristan, tell me how you feel. Can you stand? Do you think you can walk, or ride if we can find horses? Robard says we really should be on the move. Sir Hugh will no doubt find our trail soon enough, if he hasn't already."

"Do we know where we are?" I asked. "Which direction we need to go?"

"West," Maryam said.

"North," Robard said at the same time.

"You have no idea where we are, do you?" I asked.

"Yes. We most certainly do. We are in England. And for a long time we had the cliffs of Dover in view. Then, well . . . we may have drifted a bit," he said.

"A bit?"

"Quite a bit, perhaps—a lot, actually. The wind really catches the sail, and if you don't get the rudder turned correctly, you end up going . . . Never mind. We're safely home, Tristan. In England." Robard gave me his best smile.

Maryam brought us back to reality. "Regardless of where we are, we need to get moving. Tristan, can you stand? Walk?" she asked. I had been sitting by the fire, my head in my hands, wondering how far we would have to travel to reach Rosslyn. I couldn't really blame them, though. We were still alive.

"I'm not sure. Let me try," I said. Standing was going to be painful, but there was no way around it. Maryam was right. It was time for us to be under way.

I put one leg under me while Robard knelt, holding my other arm. Together we stood and the pain was only slightly less than excruciating. The world spun and I feared I might pass out. "Easy," Robard said. "Steady."

After a moment, the pain lessened and I could stand unaided. Taking a few tentative steps back and forth, I could manage a sort of shuffling walk. But at this rate, it would take me years to reach Scotland.

"Careful," Maryam said. "Getting shot by an arrow *hurts*." She stared at Robard pointedly, but he refused to meet her gaze.

"Yes, it does, I'm told. But not as much as being stabbed by a Hashshashin dagger," Robard shot back.

"We're going to need horses," I said, interrupting.

"You know, riding a horse . . ." Maryam let the words trail off.

"I know. It's going to hurt even worse. But the pain will pass. We'll never make it on foot, and I'll only slow us up," I said.

Robard and Maryam nodded in agreement. I decided it was a good idea to sit back down before I passed out.

"So how do we do that?" I asked. "Find horses."

Neither of them spoke, staring at the fire, thinking.

"Do we have any idea where we are exactly? Where in England specifically?"

Robard shook his head. "I said *sailing* is not as hard as it looks. *Navigating* is an entirely different matter. We'll just need to find the nearest town or village to find out where we are. Then we'll see about horses. You still have money?"

I nodded. I also had Sir Thomas' ring, but trading it for horses would leave a clear clue for Sir Hugh if he followed us here.

"Good. I'm not opposed to stealing, since this is something of an emergency, but it would be better for us if we had just one group chasing us at a time," he remarked.

"I say we rest here tonight and leave refreshed in the morning," Maryam suggested.

"Good idea," I said wearily. Exhaustion and pain were enveloping me again. My hip still burned and my eyes grew heavy.

Robard stood, kicking at a few of the logs on the fire with his boot. The flames died down and he banked the coals so only a slow warm glow flowed over me. He strung his bow.

"What are you doing?" Maryam asked.

"I'm going to scout around a bit," he said. "Keep an eye on things. You won't see me until tomorrow morning, so don't be alarmed. But I'll always be nearby. If there's trouble, give one of those Al Hashshashin war cries of yours. They're loud enough to wake the dead. I'll hear it and be back before you know it. Tristan, rest easy. Try not to injure yourself any further, if you don't mind."

Then as if he were a ghost, Robard disappeared into the night.

y eyes opened as dawn broke. Maryam slept on the other side of the fire with Angel curled next to her. It was too early to rise, I thought, and there was no sign of Robard. It wouldn't hurt for me to rest awhile longer.

When I opened my eyes again—surely just seconds later—Robard was standing by the fire, leaning on his bow, staring at me with a giant grin on his face.

"Good morning," he said. He surprised me and I lurched awake, straining my side. I lay back quickly with a groan.

"Don't do that!" I exclaimed.

"What?" he asked.

"Sneak up on us!"

"Who is sneaking up?" Robard made a show of raising his bow and twisting his neck around as if an attack were coming.

"Oh, for heaven's sake," I said. I braced against the boulder and lifted myself to my feet. "Did you see anything or learn where we are while you were parading about?"

"Parading? I most definitely was not! Perhaps scouting, but I don't know about parading," he said in an irritatingly cheerful tone as he knelt to warm his hands by the still-glowing coals.

"Please, Robard, I don't feel well, and your cheerfulness is making me irritable," I pleaded. My head ached and my side still burned.

Robard paid no attention. "I found a village not far from here and spoke to a smith. Told him I was on my way home from the Crusades and had gotten turned around. Friendly fellow. We're about two, maybe three days' walk south of Dover. You, however, are probably four or five days' walk," he said, pointing at my wounded hip. "So Maryam and I will meet you there." His grin told me he was joking, but I was stiff, in pain and not in the mood for comedy.

"Robard, please . . . stop . . . ," I said, my voice tinged with exasperation.

Robard laughed in response. "Ha! We couldn't have planned it better if we'd tried. Well, of course we could have hit Dover directly, I suppose, but still a remarkable feat of sailing, if I do say so myself. And if we can find horses, it'll take us even less time to get there."

"Get where?" Maryam asked groggily from the ground.

"Well, good morning, sunshine!" Robard nearly shouted.

"Ugh," Maryam said, staring up at the sky, which was overcast and gray again. Rain would be coming later in the day. "Sunshine! Pfff. I've yet to see any of it since we landed here!" She sat up and stoked the fire, and soon had water boiling in a small pot she had procured somewhere.

At Robard's mention of Dover, my mind raced.

"Dover," I muttered to myself. "Not everyone I knew and trained with left for Outremer when our regimento did. There may be squires and even knights who remember me, and they might be willing to help. If I show them Sir Thomas' letter . . ." My words trailed off. It felt like the best option. We were so close, it seemed foolish not to at least try.

"Okay," Robard agreed. "There is a village not far north of here. We should be able to get horses there, or at least find someone in the nearby countryside who has them for sale. You two start walking. Follow the coast. As soon as I can find horses, I'll catch up."

"Isn't it the first place Hugh would look?" Maryam asked. "And you," she said, looking at Robard. "I don't like you always disappearing into the woods and leaving us alone. How would we ever know if something happened to you?"

"I'm going to get the horses," Robard said, "because I'm a native who didn't grow up in a monastery and thus has no idea how to bargain. I've purchased stock before and know how to deal with horse traders. I'm less likely to be noticed. We've been waiting here for two days while Tristan recovered. We can't take the chance Sir Hugh hasn't put the word out about three wanted criminals traveling together. I'll catch up to you with the horses, and I promise we won't split up after that. At least then we'll be on horseback and have a better chance of eluding capture." Robard was trying hard to convince her. Maryam had woken up in a foul mood.

"I think Robard's plan makes sense. But go quickly," I said, removing the small bag of coins from the satchel and adding Sir Thomas' ring to it. "We need good mounts, and this is all the money I have left. If you have to use the ring . . . I . . . would rather keep it, but if you must."

Robard's hand closed over the coin purse. "I'll do my best," he said.

He handed his bow and wallet to Maryam. As we had traveled through France, after escaping from Montségur, Robard had been teaching Maryam to shoot his longbow.

"Take care of these," he said. "You're becoming quite a proficient archer. Remember, shoulders steady, feet set and breathe out when you loose."

"Robard! You might need it," she exclaimed, pushing it back to him.

He shook his head. "No. Not this time. They'll be searching for an archer fitting my description. So if I don't fit the description . . . ," he trailed off. "Besides, I have this!" He grasped the hilt of Sir Thomas' battle sword hanging from his belt.

Maryam glanced at me with a pained expression. "Robard. Please don't take this the wrong way . . . ," she said.

"What?" he said, curious.

"You know you are a gifted archer," she said.

"Of course."

"Well, you are not so talented with the sword. In fact, you are a horrible swordsman. There, I said it," she finished quickly.

"What? I am not! I can fight as well with a sword as anyone!" he nearly shouted.

He pulled the sword as if to make his case. It was a clumsy draw, though, and the point hung up on the scabbard. Then the blade became stuck and he had to push it back in and draw again. In all, about a half minute passed before the sword cleared.

"See what I mean?" Maryam said.

There was no need to let Robard's temper get the best of him, so I jumped in. "You are right, Robard. Go and return as quickly as you can. Maryam and I will start out for Dover. I'm sure you'll be able to track us. But if you lose us somehow, there is a well-trod road, called the traveler's road, west of the city, about three leagues out. We will gather there if need be." I even gave him a little salute.

"Right. Well, I'd best be on my way," he said. He tried to return the sword to the scabbard and succeeded after three attempts. Please, God, I prayed. Keep him safe until he returns to us. I crossed myself and Maryam uttered a prayer to Allah. We watched until Robard disappeared from sight.

Angel whimpered, as she always did whenever we separated, but she rolled over onto her back and Maryam gave her a good belly rub. Satisfied, she sat up and sniffed the air. I took the opportunity to walk back and forth around the campsite, testing my wounded side. Each step brought a small wave of pain, but it was bearable, and slowly I worked at returning to full strength. I remembered my dream. Sir Thomas warned me danger was coming. I had no idea what he meant. Was it that the closer I got to Scotland, the more desperate Sir Hugh would become? Was the Queen Mother trying to find me as well? Or was it that some other as yet unseen or unrealized danger awaited? Knowing our luck thus far, I wouldn't be surprised if a dragon awaited us over the next rise.

"How are you feeling?" Maryam asked, rising from her morning prayers.

"Better, thanks. Maryam, don't worry. Robard will be fine. He knows a lot more than he ever lets on. He told me when we first met that he was a poor and simple farmer. But I'm finding him much more complex. I have no doubt he'll return unharmed, with mounts for us. This will all be over soon, and you can return home."

Maryam stared off in the distance. "Home. I dared not think of it," she mumbled. But I knew she wasn't thinking of home but rather how much she wished Robard had not left us alone. In France, Robard had decided to make it back to England on his own, separating from us for a short time. Every hour he was gone, Maryam was miserable, and her joy at our reunion a few days later was palpable. Watching them since, I'd seen how much closer they'd become. Robard would look at her and a small smile would cross his face. When she had been held captive by Sir Hugh in Calais, he had nearly gone mad in his desire to save her. Neither of them thought I noticed what was happening between them, but I did.

For some reason, Maryam's worry over Robard made me think of Celia, the Cathar princess we had left behind at her mountain fortress in southern France. It had been one of the hardest things I'd ever done. On some level, I understood Maryam's feelings, for I often wondered if Celia still remembered me. I tried to push her face and smile from my mind, for the thought that she might have forgotten me already was too horrible to bear.

"Maryam," I asked. "Do you think . . ."

"What?" she prodded me.

"Nothing." Best I change the subject.

"I think Robard is right," I said. "We should get moving and follow the coast. If we're out in the open, we have less chance of walking into an ambush, plus we won't get lost that way. If we come upon any settlements, we'll turn inland and go around them.

Robard will be able to track us easily, and the quicker we get to Dover, the better." Taking the pot of tea off the fire with a stick, I kicked dirt over the coals.

"Why? Why not wait here for Robard to return? What do you think you're going to find in Dover, Tristan?" she asked. I'd seldom seen Maryam like this. Robard's absence made her uneasy. I was not sure whether it was because she felt safer when he was with us, or because her feelings for him had grown.

I thought of the Commandery, my months of living and training there, of the knights and squires and the controlled chaos of dinnertime in the main hall, of the hours of training on the fields and work, and the laughter from the squires' barracks as we fell dead tired into our beds each night. They were some of my happiest memories. Someone had to be there who would remember Sir Thomas.

"Help," I said. "I'm hoping I'll find help."

he way our luck had gone, we almost expected Robard to be captured by King's Guards or Sir Hugh's knights. Maryam and I, already on the road to Dover, would be forced to divert to where he was being held and attempt another rescue or offer Sir Hugh the Grail in exchange for his life.

However, our luck held. Maryam and I departed for Dover soon after Robard left. My wound made it impossible for us to maintain any sort of reasonable pace. Still, it was good to be on our way. Walking was exhausting, but I hoped the exercise would help me heal faster. Robard found us the following morning, camped a short distance inland from the coast.

Robard had procured two horses, both rouncies, a chestnut gelding and a roan mare. They appeared to be reasonably well trained and even tempered, though they were thin and small, unlikely to win any races.

"Only two?" Maryam asked.

"We're lucky to have them," Robard explained. "We only have a few crosslets left. But don't worry, Assassin, you can ride with me."

"Ha," Maryam said, surprising us both by swinging up on the back of the mare. "You can ride with me!"

"I told the courser I was up from Portsmouth, seeking mounts for the retinue of my thane. He wasn't much of a talker, but if he gets asked about any strangers, he'll at least send them in the wrong direction," Robard said, tossing me the money sack. I was relieved to find Sir Thomas' ring still there. Robard helped me mount the gelding, then leapt easily behind Maryam on the mare and we were quickly under way.

Robard's mood had improved greatly since we'd arrived in England. In Outremer and even in France he was often gruff and angry. Obviously he was more comfortable traveling here. And we discovered more about our friend every day. For someone who claimed to be a poor farmer, he knew his way around the world. He had left us, found a courser and returned quickly, ready for whatever next steps we needed to take. His eagerness was nearly infectious.

We sat astride our horses, gazing down at the city of Dover, having ridden in through the hills to the south. Though it had been less than a year since I'd left it, the change was dramatic. What had been a busy, bustling seaport was now eerily quiet.

"Does anyone know what today is?" I asked.

"No idea," Robard and Maryam answered almost simultaneously.

"Why?" Robard asked.

"I just wondered. The town appears empty, as if it were Sunday, or a saints' day, which might explain why it is so quiet," I said.

My horse shifted under me and my eyes worked over the city below. When I'd first arrived in Dover, the marketplace was full of people and merchants. Now most of the carts and stalls stood empty, with perhaps a quarter of the merchants hawking their wares. I spotted the spire of St. Benedict's, the church where I had left my horse Charlemagne upon first arriving here with Sir Thomas and the knights. Above the Commandery, the brown and white Templar banner flew, but the training fields behind it were empty.

"What next, Tristan?" Maryam asked.

"I'm not sure. Something has drastically changed. It is not the Dover I remember. It was lively, and full of travelers and merchants and soldiers. This Dover looks nearly dead."

"Then I say we skip our way around it and head north to Scotland. The sooner you're rid of that satchel, the better for all of us," Robard said. We sat there in silence for a while, watching the town below. I knew they were both waiting for me to take action.

"Tristan? Have you figured this all the way through yet?" Maryam finally asked.

"What do you mean?" I asked.

For a moment I felt myself tense. Since I had regained my senses, I had yet to tell Maryam or Robard what the Queen Mother had said to me in the courtyard. But I wondered if they had overheard her or if in my delirium I had revealed something. I was keeping another secret from them. It wasn't right.

"Sir Hugh. The Grail. He wants it at any cost. Do you really think handing it over to a priest in Scotland is going to stop him?" she asked.

"The Assassin is right," Robard said. "He won't stop. Even if you give it over to this Father William, he'll try to capture you or one of us and hold us hostage until you tell him where it is or until you retrieve it and trade it to him in exchange for our lives. Getting your vase to Scotland is the least of your worries."

"It's not a vase," I complained. But Robard was right. They both were.

"You understand what this means, don't you?" Robard asked.

I did, but had no desire to say it.

"He will hurt anything and everything close to you until he has what he wants," Robard went on. "It would almost be better if we found him and you let me kill him for you. He's a despicable scoundrel and I wouldn't mind." Robard was trying to be light-hearted about it, but he was also serious in his offer.

"I'm trying not to kill anyone, Robard," I said. Though my words sounded hollow, I doubted even a knight as honorable as Sir Thomas would fault me if Robard were able to put an arrow in Sir Hugh's heart from a hundred paces. Without another word, I turned my horse west and took off at a trot, but I quickly slowed the horse to a walk when the pain in my side made it impossible to keep going. In a moment they caught up to me.

"Where are we going?" he asked. "Scotland lies to the north."

"Yes, I'm well aware of Scotland's location. But there may be help for us here. Let's wait until dark. Tonight we'll pay a visit to Dover," I said.

ollowing a trail leading inland, Robard found a dense thicket where the horses could be safely hobbled for the night. It was fed by a small stream so the animals would have water, and the woods were so thick that it was unlikely our mounts would be discovered until we returned. I had advised we wait until nightfall before we entered the city, so with little else to do, each of us took turns standing watch and sleeping beneath the gently swaying trees.

At sundown, I nudged Robard with my boot. He had been softly snoring by the fire and came awake instantly. He started several different arguments all at once. "Why are we wasting time in Dover? We should be heading for Scotland straightaway. Why are we leaving the horses? What if we need to make a quick getaway? What then?" And so on. I instantly wished I'd left him asleep and ignored him for as long as possible, but the archer wouldn't stop until I finally countered his numerous opinions.

"Ideally we won't have to make a quick getaway. I just want to scout around. Maybe we can discover where Sir Hugh is and what his plans are. If we know where he is, it's to our advantage. He won't be able to sneak up on us. It's better than blundering right into him unprepared. The horses will slow us down in town. I want to be able to move quickly and hide if necessary. It's much harder to hide on a horse."

"I would think it would depend on the horse," he said, his eyes darting at me as he spoke.

"What? What would depend on the horse? You . . . stop . . . That doesn't even make sense," I stammered.

"Sure it does. I have been working on it during the ride, teaching my horse how to hide successfully," he joked. Maryam couldn't help but laugh.

I sighed in exasperation.

"How long is this going to take?" he asked. "I'm eager to reach Sherwood. The sooner we deliver your pottery, the faster I'll be home and sleeping in my own bed."

"I have no idea," I said. "It will take as long as it takes. And it's not 'pottery,' it is the Holy Cup of the Savior and the most sacred relic in the world. You shouldn't be so blasphemous."

"Bah!" said Robard as he waved his hand dismissively.

Maryam brought us back to reality. "Tristan, are you sure this is a good idea? Going into Dover, I mean. You, we, could be captured again. If Sir Hugh is there . . ."

"I know. But a few members of the original regimento I joined remained behind here when the rest of us departed for Outremer. If they're still at the Commandery, they will remember Sir Thomas and might be able to aid us," I explained again.

Maryam shook her head, knowing I couldn't be dissuaded. "If your friend Sir Hugh hasn't turned them against you," she muttered.

"Sir Hugh . . . is . . . was . . . not popular with many members of the regimento. I doubt he could persuade them all to turn against Sir Thomas' memory. But if you both are so concerned, you may stay here—"

"Oh no you don't!" Robard interrupted. "I don't intend to let you out of my sight. I've had quite enough of coming to your rescue."

Now it was my turn for mock anger. "What? When have you ever come to *my* rescue? I caught you on the cliff at Montségur, I saved you from a beating at the hands of Philippe! Well, actually it was Angel, but still. You coming to *my* rescue? I think you are sadly—"

"Enough! Goodness, the two of you argue like the old women in my village. Stop this nonsense. Let's go!" Maryam shouted at us and stomped away, leaving the cover of the woods behind and heading down the rise toward Dover.

Robard and I followed, and after a short walk we reached the outskirts of the city. The night was cold. I rubbed my hands together and wrapped them in the folds of my tunic for warmth. It would be colder before the sun rose again. There was a half moon in the sky and some of the buildings were lighted by torchlight. Candles burned in the windows of the huts and small shops, and the glow of their cook fires danced through shutters and curtains as we passed by.

We left Angel behind to guard the horses. She was napping peacefully and opened one sleepy eye when I bade her stay. She had looked at me with her intelligent eyes and, somehow understanding our need to keep the horses as safe as possible, didn't make a fuss about following us. She rolled back over and was soon asleep. The poor little mutt had been through a lot the last few days.

Off in the distance high above the city stood the castle where I'd first met King Richard more than a year ago. It felt like only yesterday when I had stood in the Great Hall while the Lionheart addressed our regimento. In other ways it felt like a lifetime since I'd last walked these streets.

"What are you thinking about?" Maryam asked.

"Nothing," I answered.

"Are you with us, squire?" Robard said, his tone somewhere between teasing and serious. "You need to be alert. I don't like this idea one bit. I'm willing to bet you my bow Sir Hugh is here, and we're likely to run into him at any moment."

"Yes. I am alert, Robard. I was just thinking," I said, pointing toward the next street. "This way. We'll head to the Commandery. It's on the other side of town."

The sky was overcast, and when the moon rose later in the evening, the clouds would cut the light. Most of the dwellings were quiet, with no firelight coming from inside. A few torches were lighted here and there, but we would be able to move about without being seen clearly, for the most part. As we walked, I found myself clenching and unclenching my hands and breathing in short bursts. My side ached, and I was certainly not going to be much help if we had to fight our way out. Had I made a mistake in bringing us here?

We darted down the alleys and the narrow passageways between buildings, trying our best to stay out of sight. Each step we took made my heart thunder in my chest. In truth, there were very few people out at this time of night and we had little difficulty passing through town largely unseen. But I felt as if danger lurked in the shadows and Sir Hugh was hiding behind every corner. Despite the cold, I was sweating. My legs grew heavy and each step took more and more effort. I kept telling myself it was only nerves and to stay alert, but I had trouble concentrating and only became more agitated.

Whenever someone appeared on the street, we behaved as if we belonged there—strolling along, talking in low tones and giving no one a reason to suspect us of anything. In a few minutes we had reached the marketplace in the center of town. It was deserted, but as we cut through the closed-up stalls, memories overtook me. I thought of the morning after Sir Thomas had introduced me to King Richard and he'd reacted so strangely. He *must* have sent the King's Guards to follow me that day. The guards had tracked me through these very streets, and were it not for the timely appearance of Sir Basil, who knows what may have happened. In hindsight, it was clear the guards had intended to do me harm.

Then later, Sir Hugh attacked me on the practice field during sword drills, and Sir Thomas had warned him to leave me alone on threat of death. When Sir Thomas had bested Sir Hugh on the fields of the Commandery, Sir Hugh had said, "I know who he is. . . ." How could he when I didn't even know who I was?

Something jerked me off my feet, and the next thing I knew I was up against the side of the building with Robard's face inches from my own. He had yanked me back into the alley after I had just absentmindedly wandered out into the street.

"What?" I groused.

"What are you doing, Tristan?" Robard asked. "You blundered out into the street without looking to see if it was clear. Are you deliberately trying to get us killed?"

"No," I said, ashamed.

"You need to be *here*, Tristan, not in Outremer or back in France or dreaming of the fair Celia," Robard commanded. I blushed when he mentioned Celia's name. It would be useless to protest that she was about the only thing I *wasn't* thinking of.

"I . . . I'm sorry," I said. And I was. Robard was absolutely right. My attention was too scattered, and my lack of focus was dangerous.

I took a deep breath and tried to push the thoughts of kings and queen mothers and King's Guards out of my head.

Robard let out an exaggerated sigh. "Sorry won't keep us out of the dungeon, squire. Let's do what we came here for, whatever it is, and get back to our horses."

"Right. Of course. I'm sorry, Robard. Come. It's not much farther." We walked on, keeping to the shadows, and a few moments later stood just down the street from the main gate of the Commandery. Peering around the corner of a darkened shop, I studied the surroundings for several minutes. No one entered or left the grounds, but it was not guarded.

"What now?" Maryam whispered.

"I'm going to sneak in and see if there is anyone there who might be able to help," I said.

"How are you going to 'sneak' in?" Robard asked incredulously.

"I don't know," I replied.

"That's what I thought," he said.

I tried hard to think of something. If I could get into the Commandery without being seen, perhaps I could find a friendly brother like Sir Westley or some of the squires I'd served with and explain my predicament. Perhaps I could even learn of Sir Hugh's whereabouts.

Several minutes passed and no one came or went from the grounds. Time to take action.

"Come on, I want the two of you to boost me over the wall," I said. "We'll go around to the rear where the training grounds are. We're less likely to be noticed there."

"Wonderful," Robard muttered, but he and Maryam followed me down the street.

"You are trying to sneak into a small fortress manned by a group of heavily armed, well-trained fighters who may have been ordered to capture you," Maryam observed. "You don't see any problems with your strategy?"

"None," I said. Without giving them time to answer, I stepped onto the street and, staying to the shadows, moved along the front of the building opposite the gate. I wanted to circle the Commandery first, to make doubly sure there was no one about.

Just then, without warning, the doors pulled open and six mounted knights rode through, Sir Hugh at their lead.

8

dove behind a two-wheeled cart parked in front of the building. It would be a miracle if they didn't see me. Casting a quick glance behind me, I found Robard and Maryam backing into the shadows of the building's recessed doorway, trying desperately to become invisible in the darkness. I lay on the ground, attempting to tighten my entire body into the tiniest size possible.

The horses pranced out of the gate, then stopped in the street. Sir Hugh's high-pitched voice was instructing the knights, but I couldn't make out what he was saying. I raised my head, peering over the top of the cart, but a sharp hiss from Maryam startled me and I ducked down again.

The clouds were backlighted by the rising moon, which was almost at its highest point in the night sky. Unfortunately the shadows along the buildings lining our side of the street were beginning to shorten. If Sir Hugh and his men did not ride off soon, we were surely done for. They would see me if they came toward us, and Robard and Maryam would not be hidden for much longer either. My breath came in short gasps and the blood pounding in my ears made it difficult to think.

The sound of horses cantering down the street was a welcome relief. I peered out at the street from beneath the cart. The column rode into my view with Sir Hugh at the lead and the brothers following two abreast, and I was overjoyed to see they were heading away from us. I was about to stand up when everything went sour.

The building secreting Maryam and Robard was a small inn. During my time in Dover it had been a raucous place filled with revelers and drunks. It had fallen on hard times like the rest of the town. No sound came from within and its windows were dark. From all appearances, it looked deserted.

Yet it was not.

Before Sir Hugh and the brothers reached the end of the street, a man opened the door and stepped out carrying a bucket full of ashes, which he must have intended to dump in the street. The door had hidden Robard from his view, but he nearly trampled Maryam. Then he spotted me lying on the ground beside the cart. He bellowed, "What is this? What are you doing here?"

Robard pushed the door shut and grasped the man with one arm, clamping his other hand over the man's mouth. The man gasped and dropped the bucket, which made a loud clanging sound when it struck the cobblestone street. He thrashed and kicked, and tried to shout out. Robard's hand muffled his cries, but not enough.

"Quiet!" Maryam whispered. "We mean you no harm!" She tried to reach out and calm him, but he continued to struggle and moaned even louder.

Keeping my eyes on Sir Hugh, I watched in horrid fascination as he raised his hand and called his horsemen to a halt. He turned his stallion and cantered back toward us.

"Run!" I shouted.

I sprang up from my spot on the ground and starting sprinting away. Robard and Maryam did not have to be told twice, and their footsteps pounded on the street behind me.

"Thieves! Thieves!" the man shrieked.

"Stop!" Sir Hugh commanded. "I demand that you stop!"

Not bloody likely.

When we reached the corner, we turned onto the main thoroughfare leading to the marketplace.

"After them!" Sir Hugh shouted. Robard and Maryam had quickened their pace and were running beside me. Every step brought burning pain down my entire leg. I would not be able to keep this up for long.

"Better think of something quick, squire!" Robard gasped. We were no match for men on horseback, and indeed, judging by the sound of their hoofbeats, our pursuers were gaining on us.

"This way!" I shouted, darting down a narrow alley that cut across our path. This area of town was mostly shops. The alley was full of barrels, small carts and other assorted implements, which required us to carefully pick our way through. But it would make it difficult for someone on horseback to follow.

The alley twisted to the right and we kept running. The sound of hoofbeats dimmed, and for a brief second I thought we'd already lost them, but I could hear shouting coming from in front of us. "They're trying to flank us!" Robard whispered.

We skidded to a stop a few paces from where the alley cut across another street.

"What now?" Maryam asked. The wound in my side was throbbing. Horses were heading toward us, but I could not determine from what direction.

Still gasping for breath, I hopped onto a nearby barrel. I could almost reach the roof of the building.

"Help me up," I said.

Robard held his hands up over his head, making a platform, and I stepped into them with my left foot and pushed up. The roof was made of timbers and I found a handhold to pull myself up. "Hurry," I said.

"You next," Robard said to Maryam.

"No, you first," she whispered back.

"What? No! No time to argue—up you go," he said, holding his hands together.

"Ha!" Maryam snorted. Instead of climbing up like I had, she backed up several paces. "What are you doing?" Robard exclaimed, trying to keep his voice from rising.

"Climbing," Maryam said. She took off, and in no more than three steps she was at full speed. Reaching the barrel, she leapt off of one foot, her other landing squarely on top of the barrel, and then vaulted herself up the side of the wall. The next thing I knew, she was beside me on the roof, reaching down to assist Robard with his climb.

Robard and I stared in wonder. "How . . . did you . . ." I couldn't finish. Every time Maryam did something remarkable, I thought she couldn't surprise me any more. Yet she continued to do just that.

We could hear men coming down the alley. Maryam and I reached down to Robard, and with each of us taking an arm he pulled himself up to the roof. The three of us lay still, waiting for the knights to appear out of the shadows. I had just enough time to draw my sword, and gripped it tightly in my hand as two Templars appeared. Their white tunics with red crosses emblazoned on the chest were easy to spot in the muted moonlight. They walked cautiously with their swords held in front of them, checking every possible hiding place.

We watched in silence as they strolled right beneath us. I could see the plumes of their breath rising up to the cold night sky. Had I wished it, I could almost have reached out and conked both of them on the head with the hilt of my sword.

The entrance to the alley was about thirty paces away. They waited there until Sir Hugh and the other men arrived, still astride their horses.

"What do you mean, they aren't here?" he demanded. "You must have missed them. Search again." The two men looked at each other a brief moment, then dutifully turned and retreated the way they'd come. I hoped Sir Hugh would ride off to begin searching another section of town, but he and his men remained.

A small creaking sound caught my ear and I sensed movement to my right. I had been so intent on Sir Hugh that I had failed to realize that Robard had risen to one knee and managed to string his bow. He held it up, an arrow nocked, taking aim.

Sir Hugh was only partially visible, the wall of the building opposite us hiding most of him from our view. It was far too risky a shot, and I reached over Maryam, who lay between us, and grabbed his arm. "Shh," he whispered at me, trying to twist his arm free from my grasp.

"Robard," I whispered, my voice so low that he had to strain to hear me, "don't shoot."

"Why not?" he whispered back. "When he moves back into sight, I think I can take him. We could end this here."

"Can you shoot them all? Those are his men. We're trapped up here. What if you miss? They could keep us here forever or even burn the building down with us on top of it," I explained.

"Quiet," Maryam commanded. "You two idiots are going to get us caught. I am not going to be thrown into another dungeon!"

Robard frowned and lowered his bow. "You'd probably just be hanged again," he whispered. Maryam shook her head.

We waited, the minutes passing by. I wondered about the Grail. It had remained silent so far, but I wondered if it also pulled Sir Hugh to it somehow. I could not imagine God would allow such a thing, but yet there Sir Hugh waited, not more than a stone's throw away, looking like something was holding him in place.

Finally, the other two knights rode up and reported to Sir Hugh. He was furious.

"Imbeciles. I'm certain it was the squire. I'd swear to it. He came here looking for me."

"But Marshal, it could have been anyone. Perhaps some thieves—"

"No! It was them!" Sir Hugh cried. "Continue the search. They are here somewhere!"

"Yes, sir," the knight said. All of them spurred their horses and moved off down the street. All except for Sir Hugh. I was about to stand up when he reappeared at the entrance of the alley. He had dismounted and, no doubt remembering Robard and his bow, kept himself hidden, peering cautiously around the corner. He studied the alley intently for several minutes. He looked at the ground and the walls, then raised his gaze to study the rooftops on either side. I could sense each of us consciously flattening ourselves against the roof. I kept one eye on him and gripped my sword so tightly that I thought I would break the hilt.

It was unsettling. I could have sworn he was staring right at me. I strained hard to hear the musical sound of the Grail. But it was silent. No vibration, nothing. Sir Hugh's eyes never wavered. The tension was unbearable, and I momentarily thought of ending this now. I would leap to the ground and Sir Hugh and I would have at it until one of us was dead.

My muscles twitched in anticipation, and just as I was about stand and leap, Sir Hugh abruptly disappeared from view. We heard the sound of his horse trotting away in the darkness.

It took a few seconds before any of us were able to breathe normally.

"What has gotten into him? Did you see how he stood there? I thought he was looking right at us," Robard said.

"Yes, it was very strange," Maryam agreed.

"Let's go," I said.

"Go where?" Robard asked. "They're looking for us. The streets aren't safe for us any longer."

"Then we won't use the streets," I said.

Giving my friends no time to talk me out of it, I stood and backed away from the edge of the roof. Then I ran forward as hard as I could and leapt into the air.

s it turned out, I had misjudged the distance. By a great deal, actually. I had intended to leap across the alley to the next building and then move along the rooftops, avoiding Sir Hugh and the knights tracking us below. But my jump was just short, and I slammed hard into the edge of the roof and wall. The timber and stone gave no ground, and pain flared in my wounded side. I thought I would surely pass out and fall and break my neck.

"Dear God," I heard Robard mutter.

"What has gotten into him?" Maryam asked quietly.

"I don't know. He won't let me shoot Sir Hugh. Now he's trying to jump from roof to roof like a wounded rabbit. And he's likely woken everyone who lives in both of these buildings and for several leagues around."

I tried to ignore them, but I was in a slight predicament. My grip on the roof was loosening and I tried to dig my feet into the wall to pull myself up, but to no avail. I ran my hands over the roof timbers, but there was no place I could gain even a fingerhold. My boots dug furiously at the wall.

"Um. I could use a little help," I said quietly.

"So it would appear," Robard answered.

"Perhaps I wasn't clear," I said, "in that I require *immediate* help."

I heard nothing for a few moments except for exaggerated sighs and the rustle of feet, and then both Robard and Maryam landed deftly on the roof to either side of me. They each grasped an arm and pulled me up.

I bent at the waist, struggling to breathe and wishing for something that would quell the fire in my burning side. "It was a good plan," I said. "If we keep to the rooftops, we'll be less likely to be spotted. I just . . . My wound . . . My jump was a little off."

"A little," Robard said.

"We should leave," Maryam said. "There are noises coming from inside this building. I'm sure whoever is inside heard us . . . you, rather . . . land on their roof."

There was no time to defend myself. We crossed over and jumped to the next building. Many of the structures had only a few feet between them. Some allowed us to merely step from one roof to the next. Robard had his bow at the ready. Maryam did not draw her daggers yet, not wanting the moon to reflect off of them. I kept my sword sheathed for the same reason.

We went as far as we could, back to the marketplace. The streets widened there and we could go no farther by rooftop. We found a darkened alcove facing the marketplace and climbed down. It appeared deserted, and Robard and Maryam were in favor of making our way back to our horses as quickly as we could. But something made me cautious. We had lost track of Sir Hugh and his men, and I did not want to blunder upon them unaware.

I had learned what I came for. Sir Hugh was here in Dover. He might have other knights patrolling the countryside. Maybe even some of the King's Guards. But he was the one who would look the hardest, leaving nothing to chance. No empty barn or cave or hole where we might hide would go unsearched. At least he wouldn't be sneaking up on us. We could make a better decision about how to reach Rosslyn knowing his whereabouts. If we weren't caught here, of course.

Robard nocked an arrow. "Robard, one thing," I said. "These knights. Many of them are just following orders. Please don't kill any of them if you can avoid it."

"Hmm" was all Robard said as he readied himself for a potential attack. We weren't safe yet.

The marketplace sat at the intersection of Dover's two main thoroughfares. The streets widened and were covered with cobblestones. A ring of buildings surrounded it and at night, while it was empty, I discovered sound carried very well. Though we stepped lightly, every noise we made echoed, and I couldn't imagine how we could pass through unheard.

We kept close to the buildings ringing the square and used their shadows and doorways to hide us. But at some point we would have to cross one of the wide streets and would be exposed. We had no choice.

When we stepped out of the shadows and sprinted across the nearest street, the horsemen were on us in an instant. Sir Hugh had planned well, keeping his men out of sight and far down the thoroughfare. When we crossed, we were silhouetted and clearly visible. The knights charged forward, and the noise of their advance sounded like a thunderstorm.

Robard stood and took aim at the closest man. He calmly fired, and we heard a scream and the sound of mail and armor clanking to the ground. I hoped Robard hadn't killed him. These men had been deceived by Sir Hugh, I told myself, not wanting to live with the guilt of killing or injuring innocent men.

There were two mounted men on each street leading into the marketplace. Shouts and commands rang in the air, and the sound of hooves clattering on cobblestone grew louder.

"Robard!" I shouted as one of them was almost on us. Robard's arrow whizzed past the man, who ducked behind his horse's neck. Robard pulled another shaft from his wallet, but we had no time. Then an empty wheeled cart came shooting into the street between us and the knight's horse reared, nearly colliding with it. He was instantly unhorsed and fell hard on the ground, stunned.

"Hurry!" Maryam shouted. Her quick thinking had saved us. We ran into the center of the marketplace, dashing through the maze of closed stalls and empty carts. The knights would have to dismount to catch us, but we were also trapped. I caught a glimpse of Sir Hugh circling around us on horseback, commanding his men to dismount and follow on foot. Robard sent an arrow in his direction, and Sir Hugh leapt off his horse with a squawk. He hid on the other side of the stallion, giving Robard nothing to aim at.

"What are we going to do?" Robard asked. "We're trapped."

I tried to think of our next move.

"What if he sends one of his men to the Commandery to bring help?" Maryam asked.

"If there is even a full regimento there, I hope he has them out searching the countryside. . . . Regardless, they have all of the ways out covered. I believe they'll try to wait us out. They won't want to face an archer up close. I think we're relatively safe for the moment," I said.

I closed my eyes, trying hard to concentrate. Robard stood, bow at the ready, and I counted only a few arrows left in his wallet. Not a good thing. Not a good thing at all. My thoughts were interrupted by Robard's shout, "Look out!" He pushed me roughly to the side, and a crossbow bolt thudded into a wooden post right where I'd been kneeling. I hated crossbows.

We found what cover we could as several more bolts flew at us.

"Robard, stay down," I said. "If they try to draw you out . . . We can't lose you."

"I'm not going anywhere, squire, and neither are you, and . . . Tristan . . . where is Maryam?"

From my hiding place, I glanced around me in every direction, but she was nowhere to be found. She was either excellent at hiding or had disappeared into thin air. "I don't know," I answered. "Maryam? Maryam, where are you?" I called quietly.

"Confound it!" Robard exclaimed. "What is that Assassin up to? If she gets herself caught again . . ." Robard tried to sound angry, but he was worried. I knew he would fight the knights with his bare hands before he'd let any harm come to her.

"Perhaps she's finding an escape route," I said hopefully. "We need to get out of here. Maryam can more than take care of herself."

We remained hidden from the knights' view as best we could. Our enemies appeared comfortable with keeping us pinned down by crossbows. They fired a shot in our direction on occasion, but we were well concealed. Robard had no clear shot or time to stand and draw, so we waited.

"Maybe they've caught her," Robard mused, concern in his voice.

"No. If they had, Sir Hugh would be using her as a means to get us to surrender. He doesn't have her."

Robard muttered quiet curses under his breath. Our situation was beginning to wear on him.

"You should have let me shoot Sir Hugh in the alley," he complained bitterly.

I said nothing. It was time to act.

"Let's go," I said. "Waiting gets us nothing. We have to get out of here somehow."

My wound made bending at the waist painful, but standing upright meant instant death, so I crouched as best I could and scrambled toward the south end of the marketplace. A bolt skittered across the cobblestone in front of me, and I dove behind a cart.

Robard landed beside me an instant later. "We're wasting time," he muttered.

I tried to rise to get a view of where the knights had placed themselves, but another bolt bit into the wood just inches from my face, and I ducked again.

"They're getting closer," I yelped.

"I say we rush them!" Robard said through gritted teeth, anger at our situation beginning to get the best of him.

Then, though I would not have wished it in this manner, our deliverance arrived. From out of the darkness a fiery torch came spinning our way, followed quickly by another. The first landed harmlessly on the cobblestone and burned out, but the other clattered against a canvas-covered stall, and the material began to smolder, then burn. Sir Hugh was willing to burn down the marketplace to get to us. I wanted to rush and put it out before it caught, not wishing some poor vendor to lose his livelihood, but I held fast, for fear of the crossbowmen.

The breeze fanned the flames. In a few short moments the wood frame of the stall caught as well. Then the next stall caught, and a full-on conflagration took hold.

"Robard," I said, "this is our chance! Wait for the smoke to thicken a little, then move off toward the south end." When the time came and the air was dense with the smell of fire, Robard stood and aimed his bow.

"Robard . . . what . . ." But he loosed his arrow before I could finish, and an instant later came the answering cry of agony where it found its mark. He quickly ducked as two bolts flew through the air where he'd stood just moments before.

"How did you . . . ," I asked. Wondering how he could hit a target he couldn't see.

"I measured where he stood and marked it in my memory," he explained. "That's one less knight. I suggest we move. You're looking weaker, Tristan. Can you make it?"

"This way," I said, ignoring his question, for in truth my side ached miserably. But with the smoke swirling around us and the flames licking the night sky, I ran in my crablike gait from stall to stall. With any luck, we'd have a few precious seconds before our movement was revealed.

We paused behind a large vegetable cart and waited. We were nearly to the very end of the marketplace and the flames were moving toward us. With the fire behind us we had no other option. The blaze cast a glow in the darkness, and beyond us on the street we could see two knights guarding the nearest exit, crossbows ready, waiting for us to show ourselves. If we rushed them, they would shoot us down before we took a step. And if Robard stood and drew his bow, he might get one of them, but the other would have a clear shot at him.

I coughed as the smoke thickened. The knights strained to find where the sound had come from over the crackling noise.

Then our luck turned. From out of the night came shouts of alarm. It was the townspeople. "Fire! Fire!" rang through the night. And down the street, in the shadows beyond, I spotted movement as dozens of men and women rushed toward the marketplace.

"Robard, this is our chance," I said.

"What about Maryam?"

"One thing at a time." I grabbed hold of the handle on the cart we were hiding behind and pushed. Robard joined in, and the wheels spun as we steered it directly toward the knights twenty yards away. Distracted by the gathering crowd, they didn't notice us at first, but then one turned as we were almost upon him and fired his crossbow. The bolt bounced harmlessly off the wooden cart, but his companion's shot bit hard into the wood, next to my hand. I gasped in alarm and pushed harder, the cart gaining speed. With no time to span their crossbows, the knights dropped them to the ground and were about to draw their swords when we crashed into them.

We were immediately surrounded by a crowd of frantic Doverites, clamoring and shouting. I spotted Sir Hugh astride his horse, trying to force his way through the crowd to reach us.

"The knight there, on horseback, he's responsible for the fire!" I shouted, pointing frantically.

One man looked at me, confused and upset. "Him! Him!" I shouted, pointing at Sir Hugh again. "He ordered the marketplace burned!" A few men heard me and took off after him. Sir Hugh was trying desperately to rally the remaining knights to come after us, but the whole area was a sea of confusion, with more people pouring into the streets every second. At least now there was an angry crowd between him and us.

Robard and I ran, picking our way through the crowd. Robard still held his bow at the ready, and I had drawn my sword. He shouted and cursed, and his near madness gave us a widened path through the teeming mass of people storming toward the fire. Some were carrying buckets of water, and I prayed they could control the flames before the fire spread farther into the town.

I cast a quick glance over my shoulder and found Sir Hugh still urging his horse through the crowd. He held his sword high above his head, as if commanding the masses to part, but his words were drowned out in the chaos. In our attempt to escape, I had lost count of how many knights were still in fighting shape, but we remained outnumbered.

"We're never going to make it!" I yelled to Robard. "Once he clears the crowd, he'll ride us down!

"Robard, there!" I exclaimed. A riderless horse belonging to one of Sir Hugh's men wandered toward us, then skittered away, spooked by the advancing flames. "Come on!" We sprinted toward it, and I clutched the reins and managed to claw my way into the saddle as Robard climbed up behind me.

Slowly the crowd parted and I urged the horse onward.

"Tristan!" I heard my name shouted over the noise surrounding me. And then came a familiar ululating war cry.

"Look!" I said to Robard.

And there was Maryam, standing upright on the back of her horse lest someone in the dizzying crowd attempt to pull her from the saddle. She was leading our other mount behind her, and I could hear Angel barking madly. The crowd parted like water before Maryam's thundering horses. She reined to a stop a few paces in front of us and dropped into the saddle of her horse with practiced ease. Angel ran back and forth between Robard and me. I praised her for so admirably guarding the horses.

"I would suggest we ride," Maryam said, smiling.

10

obard took the spare horse and we turned them south and steered our way through the crowd. A quick glance told me Sir Hugh was still occupied with the mass of people, many of them angry at him for starting the fire.

"Hurry! And stay low! They still have crossbows!" I shouted above the noise. We could not easily gallop with dozens upon dozens of citizens still rushing toward the center of town. Robard cursed and bellowed and exhorted everyone in our path to make way.

"Let us pass! Out of our way! We have urgent business with the King!" he shouted. The King? We pushed and cajoled our way along, and I looked back to see a knight on horseback bringing his crossbow to bear.

"Behind us! Down!" I hollered as loud as I could. The bolt whizzed between Robard and me and into the crowd. I heard a cry of pain and the people gave way to find an old man, lying in the street, the small shaft sticking out of his shoulder. The townspeople were confused. First their marketplace was set ablaze and now someone was shooting them down in cold blood.

"Go! Keep going!" I shouted, resisting the urge to stop and aid the man. Sir Hugh was gaining, and our presence would only endanger more innocents.

"It's the man over there!" I shouted, turning in the saddle and pointing at the knight who had fired. "He did this to your fellow!" The crowd was in a confused frenzy and easy to manipulate. Two dozen people surged around my horse, charging down the street toward the knight on horseback. Though the man was a Templar, someone these folks might even know, they had witnessed what happened and wanted vengeance.

Maryam and Angel were farther ahead of us and free of the worst part of the riotous mass of people. Before long the three of us cleared them as well. We gave rein to our horses, needing to put some distance between us and Sir Hugh and his men. In a few moments we had reached the outskirts of Dover and entered the wooded countryside.

"We're headed south!" Robard shouted over the pounding hooves.

"We need to get away first and worry about direction later," I answered. The night sky would make it difficult to spot any pursuit until we could hear them, and by then they would be almost upon us. The terrain was rolling and filled with thick trees that required us to go much more slowly than I would have wished, but we could not risk running headlong into a low-hanging tree branch.

We climbed a hill lying roughly two leagues from Dover and stopped in the tree line for a moment. The moon still shone behind the cloud cover, so there was just enough light to guide us. We rested there a moment with our horses breathing hard. Angel dropped to the ground, panting, staring off the way we had come.

"This is too close to town," Maryam said. "They will be upon us—"

She was interrupted by Angel, who jumped to her feet, her body rigid and a low growl sounding in her throat. She paced a few steps and stopped, cocking her head to the side.

"Someone's coming," Robard said. And indeed off in the distance I could just make out the sounds of horses and the shouts of men. Sir Hugh and his remaining knights had freed themselves from the angry crowd and were after us.

We rode off, trying hard to make a difficult trail for them to follow.

"They are better mounted!" Robard exclaimed over the sound of hoofbeats. "It won't be long until they overtake us!" He was right. With the exception of the knights' horse I rode, Robard's and Maryam's animals were smaller and much less hardy than the warhorses ridden by the pursuing knights. What we gained in their ability to maneuver more easily through the wooded countryside was lost by the greater speed and endurance of our enemies' chargers.

"You better think of something quick!" Maryam yelled. "My poor horse is about to give out."

We rode down the edge of another rise, and off to our left, I spotted a heavily overgrown thicket, dense with shrubs and saplings and evergreens. Though it was winter, these trees still held dead leaves, and the ground cover would hide us well.

"Hold!" I said, reining my horse to a stop. "This way." I steered us into the thicket. Luckily we had ridden over some of the same ground on our trip into Dover. And I remembered a small ravine cutting through the forest floor not far ahead. If I was lucky, maybe I could trick Sir Hugh.

71

"The two of you wait here," I said. "Keep the horses and your-selves hidden." Maryam and Robard raised no argument and dis-mounted quickly. I took the satchel from my shoulder and tossed it to Robard. "If I don't come back, if Sir Hugh catches me, you know what you must do. Take it to Father William at the Church of the Holy Redeemer in Rosslyn. Don't come for me. He'll kill me anyway. He must not have this."

"What are you going to do?" Maryam asked.

"Don't worry. I have a plan." I smiled. "Come on, Angel." I turned the horse and started to trot away. "Robard, keep an arrow ready. You'll hear me coming back to the thicket before you can see me in this light. I'll yell 'Beauseant'—that way you'll know it's me. All right?"

"How will I know it isn't Sir Hugh hollering 'Beauseant' as he's about to charge us? You Templars love that word. You think you're all such great fighters. What if—"

"Robard!" I nearly yelled, trying to keep my voice under control.

"What?" he answered. Robard often became incessantly chatty when he was fighting. Or about to fight. Or finished fighting.

"Just keep alert. I won't be gone long."

Angel and I left them there in the woods and made our way back to the point where we'd cut away toward the thicket. I turned the horse and pushed him hard, hoping I wouldn't get lost in the dark. Along the way, I made no effort to disguise my route, snap-ping the branches off of passing trees and steering him through muddy ground whenever I could find it. Whenever I stopped to listen, I heard no one, but I knew they were coming and had an advantage with Angel at my side. She would hear and smell them long before they reached me.

We rode through another dense copse of trees. The muted moonlight revealed the entrance to the small ravine cutting through the forest floor, and I hoped to use it to our advantage. Without giving myself enough time to question my plan, I steered the horse down the steep slope and called for Angel to follow. We navigated the twisting gorge until we found a suitable spot. Time was our enemy. It would only be a few minutes until they tracked me here.

Sir Hugh was mad in his pursuit of me and desperate to recover the Grail. But I also believed he would be cautious. For one thing, though I had made a thorough effort to lead them directly here, he could not surmise which of us lay waiting in the darkness, and it might just be Robard with his longbow. His timidity would give me a few extra minutes. All the time I needed for my scheme to work.

The ravine was rocky, pocked with boulders and scrub trees and bushes. I walked forward a few yards until I found what I was looking for. A tree branch had fallen into the ravine from the forest above. It was about six feet long and perfect for my plan.

With my sword I hacked it in half. Ripping a length of cloth from my tunic, I lashed the branch together into a crude cross, and with a few more strips managed to tie it firmly onto the saddle so the two "arms" stuck up in the air like the arms on a headless man. Quickly I shrugged out of my brown servant's tunic, draping it over the tied-down branches. From a distance, it would appear as if I were still mounted on the horse.

Angel growled again, peering back down the ravine. The knights were coming. I wrapped the reins around the pommel of the saddle and waited. Behind me came the sound of horses and the soft clinking sound of chain mail. I closed my eyes. My thought was to convince them that we had separated and that Robard the archer waited here ready to bring doom upon them with his bow. In my mind I concentrated on remembering the sound of Robard's speech. His was a shade deeper than mine. Finally, when I was ready, I lowered my voice and shouted out to the approaching men.

"Come ahead! I'll spoon-feed you goose feather and birch straight from the bow of a King's Archer! I won't surrender and you won't take me alive!" The movement and noise down the ravine stopped as they paused to consider my comments.

"What's the matter? No taste for the longbow?" I shouted.

Still no sound.

"Then try to catch me!" I yelled, and gave the horse a sharp smack on the rump. It leapt forward, careering down the ravine, my tunic flapping in the breeze.

"Come on, Angel," I whispered. We moved another few yards ahead and found a small collection of boulders and shrubs large enough for us to hide behind. We would be invisible to anyone approaching from the opposite direction.

The sound of my horse grew fainter. The woods were almost still. But then came the creak of leather and the plodding steps of horses. They had heard my mount ride away and were coming to investigate.

With my sword in my hand and Angel quivering with silent rage beside me, we waited. Slowly, the sound of the riders drew nearer. I could not risk a look over the boulders shielding us. Any movement might be noticed.

Finally a single rider appeared. He was not more than ten yards away, but he kept his eyes forward, looking for an ambush. Angel's body shook and I held her with my free hand, silently imploring her to remain still. He passed us by, never even glancing in my direction. Then the next rider appeared, then another.

I had failed to notice it in those first tense moments, but from all around me came the gentle humming sound of the Grail. Sir Hugh's men were so close to me that I almost could have reached out and tapped each of them on the shoulder. And as it had so many times before, the music enveloped me like a blanket. I knew then that I was safe. They would not find me here. Their horses would not catch my scent and whinny in alarm. Their eyes would work the shadows of the rocks and roots lining the gorge, but they would never see me. I believed it would be possible for me to walk out of the ravine right in front of Sir Hugh and he would see nothing. But in all these many months I had yet to tempt the miracle of deliverance the Grail had brought to me so many times. I would not start now.

The knight riding point reined up and the others stopped, slowly and cautiously looking about. How many were there? I could hear the quiet murmur of conversation between them. I heard the sound of hoofbeats above and on either side of the ravine. Sir Hugh had sent some of his men to follow the ravine from the top.

I heard Sir Hugh's voice. He had stayed up there, where he would hope to find himself safe from arrows.

"Anything?" he shouted.

"No, sire," one of them replied.

"He must have ridden off," Sir Hugh pondered. "Move out!"

They spurred their horses and soon disappeared from my sight. I let out a huge sigh of relief. I counted to one hundred, waiting to make sure they did not double back to confirm I hadn't hidden from them. Then I counted to one hundred again, just to be doubly safe, before Angel and I hurried back through the ravine and toward the thicket where we had left Maryam and Robard. I had ridden some distance, and it took nearly half an hour to make our way back.

As we neared the hiding spot, I remembered Robard's itchy fingers. The last thing I needed was to surprise them and take an arrow for my trouble. When I was fifty paces away, I called out quietly, "Beauseant!" There was no reply.

"Beauseant!" Still no response.

"Robard! Maryam, where . . ." The words died in my throat as from my right came a blur and something crashed into me, knocking me harshly to the ground. My face went hard against the dirt and the breath rushed from my lungs. Someone pulled my head back, and something cold and sharp was placed against my neck.

"Maryam, it's me, Tristan," I said through gritted teeth.

"Stand up slowly." Robard's voice came from somewhere above me, but I couldn't see him with my head pushed into the dirt.

"It's me. Beauseant? Remember?" I coughed.

Maryam released me and I groaned in pain, standing slowly. When fully erect, I found I faced Robard's bow, drawn taut, the arrow pointed at my chest. He lowered it slowly.

"It's you!" he said happily.

"Who did you expect?" I replied, rubbing my side where my wound started a fresh round of burning after being thrown to the ground.

"We didn't recognize you without your tunic. Thought maybe Hugh had sent someone back looking like you, or maybe tortured you so you would tell him where we waited," he explained as he returned the arrow to his wallet.

"And this would all happen in the short time I've been gone?" I asked incredulously.

"Never can tell," he said. "He's a slippery one, that Hugh. Better to be safe."

"Well, he didn't capture or torture me. In fact I got rougher treatment from my two supposed friends," I said sarcastically, rubbing my wounded side. "And you!" I said, looking sternly at Angel. "No warning at all? You couldn't growl or bark to let me know I was about to be attacked?" Angel stared at me with a cocked head, then wagged her tail. Of course she wouldn't bark at Robard or Maryam. She looked at me as if to say, "You should have known."

Robard and Maryam shared a horse again, and with a groan I was able to climb up onto my mine. We rode north this time. There was no doubt Sir Hugh and his men would catch my horse. I wanted to be as far away as possible before they backtracked.

The ride was still difficult through the thick woods, but before long we found a shallow stream and rode along it for several leagues. It would hide our tracks and make it more difficult to follow us. The moon was sinking behind the clouds and it would be daylight soon. We needed to decide: keep riding and risk someone spotting us, or go to ground and give Sir Hugh time to catch up.

"Do you think we've lost him?" Robard asked after we'd ridden for a while.

I gave him my answer by digging my heels into the side of my horse and urging him on. If we had lost Sir Hugh, it wasn't for long. Of that I was sure.

e rode through the remainder of the night, not daring to stop except to rest briefly and water the horses. Robard took the lead most of the way, and rode with his bow strung and held across the pommel of his saddle. All the excitement in Dover had weakened me considerably. My wound ached, and before long every step of my horse sent a jolt of pain through my side.

When we were safely beyond the city, we turned back north, riding at an easy pace, giving the horses a rest, and following a well-marked but little-traveled trail through the forest. Near daybreak, we rounded a bend and found a crude wooden bridge crossing over a fairly wide stream. The area around us had grown marshy and wet, and the bridge was built in a perfect spot, spanning the deepest run of the water and leading to dry ground on the other side. It was made of rough plank and wide enough for a man on horseback to pass, but not much wider. Robard cantered up onto the bridge. We all nearly died from fright when a man suddenly appeared at the other end. He was tall, gigantic even, cloaked in a black tunic and simple leggings with a cowl obscuring his face. In one giant hand he held a wooden staff, and his other hand was held out.

"HALT!" he commanded.

Robard's horse spooked, nearly rearing, and he fought to bring it under control. They both could have plunged into the murky water below. With no room to turn around, Robard slowly backed up, until he was off the bridge.

"Who are you? Why do you order us to halt?" he shouted.

"This is my bridge. If you wish to cross, you must pay a toll!" the mysterious man shouted back. His voice sounded familiar and pulled at a string of my memory, but it was vague. Unfortunately Robard was already losing his temper.

"A toll? Pay to cross? Not bloody likely!" he shouted.

"Then come forward at your own risk," the man replied. "You'll not pass unless you pay. Two crosslets each!"

"Robard, let's not bother with this. We can head farther north and find another place to ford the stream," I pleaded.

"Nonsense! I don't believe him for an instant. Toll bridge, my arse! I'll not be bullied by some would-be troll who dares me to cross a stream. This isn't the Holy Land, it's my home country, and I'll not stand for it." Robard leapt from the back of his horse and handed the reins to Maryam.

"Robard, what are you doing?" she asked. "Tristan is right. This isn't worth it. We can find another place to cross upstream."

"I won't be but a minute," he said. He removed his bow and wallet, hanging them on the saddle, and drew Sir Thomas' battle sword, which I was still too weak to carry. He marched up to the bridge and walked slowly toward the center, shouting all the way.

"All right, you miserable pile of polecat dung! Charge me to cross a bridge, will you? I think not!"

The man at the other end walked toward Robard slowly and unafraid, his staff tapping lightly on the wooden planks. Maryam and I sucked in our breath—he was huge, the biggest man I'd ever seen and nearly a full head taller than Robard.

"Oh no," Maryam said.

"Oh . . . yes . . . ," I said. And then I shouted, "Robard! Wait! Come back!" For as the man reached the center of the bridge, he removed his cowl and there stood John Little, the Dover black-smith who had forged my sword and saved me from the ruffians set upon me by the King's Guards.

But Robard didn't hear my cry. Instead he raised the sword above his head and with a mighty yell went charging forward.

Cringing, I leapt from my horse, hobbling as best I could after Robard, desperate to save my friend from the thrashing coming his way. But it was too late. Robard rushed ahead, screaming at the top of his lungs. John Little stood silently, staff held loosely in both hands, and watched Robard's charge with a slightly bemused expression on his face.

When he was a few feet away from the giant man, Robard reared back and unleashed a mighty swing. The sword swept forward, and momentarily I feared he would connect and slay poor John.

But with an agility that belied his great size, John Little easily ducked the swing, and his staff flicked out like a serpent's tongue, hooking Robard in the back of the knees. Robard went down in a heap, and John put his foot on the blade, holding it fast. With his staff, he pressed down on Robard's chest, pinning him to the bridge.

"As I said. Two crosslets each," John Little said quietly.

"Wait! Stop!" I cried. But my shout was drowned out by the sound of Maryam's devilishly loud war cry. She nearly knocked me off the bridge as she went hurtling past, her daggers gleaming.

"Maryam, NO!" I yelled, and just managed to snatch her tunic as she ran by. She stopped short in my grasp and spun, eyes blazing, ready to fight me if necessary.

"What . . . Let me go!" she yelled, pulling me along as she wiggled her way toward the center of the bridge.

"Everyone stop!" I shouted. Maryam's eyes were full of confusion, and John stared at me with rapt concentration. Only Robard fought on, still squirming beneath the foot and staff of the giant.

I quickly drew my short sword and held it out hilt first toward the blacksmith. "John Little? You are a friend of Sir Thomas Leux. You made this sword for me, last spring, in Dover." I raised it higher so he could get a better view of it. "My name is Tristan, of St. Alban's. . . . I am . . . was Sir Thomas' squire. Remember? I brought his stallion Dauntless for you to reshoe and those two ruffians attacked me?"

"Yes. I remember you," he said quietly. John stepped back and released Robard, who remained on his back for the moment.

"Little John. You told me everyone calls you Little John," I went on.

Robard rolled to his feet. "You know this scoundrel?" he asked.

Before I or anyone could answer, Robard suddenly went flying through the air and landed with a resounding smack in the stream.

Little John had stepped forward, catlike, and with his staff as a lever lifted Robard off the ground, flipping him into the water. He had moved so quickly, I wondered if my eyes had deceived me. Robard came up sputtering and grabbed the bridge for support. He was cursing, and Maryam, who had grown calm as suddenly as she had been ready to fight, had to stifle a laugh.

Little John shook his head. "No need for name calling," he said quietly.

"Fine, you've made your point. We'll cross elsewhere," Robard said. "Will you help me up or will that cost two crosslets as well?" He held his left hand out to the giant.

"As long as you've learned your lesson," John said, grasping Robard's hand. He pulled and Robard braced his feet against the bridge timbers, letting John raise him out of the water. But when he was nearly halfway up, Robard's other hand shot out, grabbing John behind his right knee. Robard pulled hard, and as the big man's knee collapsed, his weight pulled him forward. Before any of us knew it, Robard had thrown the giant over his shoulder and into the water. It was John's turn to come up sputtering.

"Know this, Big John or Giant Man or Little Tiny Lad or whatever you call yourself. I am *Robard Hode* of Sherwood and no one to be trifled with. I'll not pay your toll and I'll not be thrown into a stream by the likes of you without getting my satisfaction, are we clear?"

Little John roared, and with frightening speed he lifted himself onto the bridge and retrieved his fallen staff. I rushed across the bridge and, without thinking, put myself between the two dripping wet combatants.

"Stop this now!" I commanded. "Robard, cease! Little John is a friend. This is a huge misunderstanding!" Trying to keep them apart was like standing between two prancing bulls, and I feared all three of us would tumble off the bridge. Eventually the steam went out of them and they stood quiet, if not quite placid.

"Little John," I said, shaking his hand, "it is good to see you!"

"And you, Tristan. Tell me, why are you not with Sir Thomas?" he asked.

With as little detail as possible, I told him what had happened to us since he and I had last met in Dover. When I related what I feared of Sir Thomas' fate, he bowed his head and went still a moment.

"A good man, that one," he said. "I pray God watches over his soul."

"John, why are you here? What happened to your smithy in Dover?" I asked him.

"Hmph. My smithy? The Lionheart's brother John took care of that. Come. I've a camp not far from here. There isn't much but I'll share it with you. Even you, *Robard Hode* of Sherwood," he said, shooting him a less than friendly look.

"I hardly think so——" Robard sputtered, but I put my hand on his chest and shushed him.

"That would be wonderful. We've had . . . a . . . what you could call a very eventful day, and we could use the rest," I said. Without another word, Little John retreated in the direction from which he'd come. We gathered up our gear and horses and followed as he disappeared into the thick woods, Robard fuming and muttering curses under his breath the whole way. Angel took the lead, content to sniff at the ground and follow Little John's scent.

In a short while, we arrived at his camp. The fire was stoked and his tunic and other wet clothing dried on a bush nearby. He had changed into a loose-fitting cloak the size of a ship's sail. An iron kettle full of pottage warmed over the fire. It was quite inviting.

He had placed several cut sections of logs near the fire and bade us sit.

"I don't have much, but let the pottage simmer for a while and I'll be happy to share." John sat on a log, his hands holding his knees. Angel sniffed lightly at John's leg and then leapt up into his lap and enthusiastically licked his face.

"Whoa! What have we here?" he exclaimed. He scratched Angel behind the ears and she flopped onto her back so John could rub her belly. Her head lolled over and I swear she locked her eyes directly on Robard, who paced back and forth behind Maryam and I while we sat on the logs near the fire.

"Traitorous beast," he muttered under his breath.

"John, what happened in these last few months to make you leave Dover?" I asked.

"When Richard departed for the Holy Land, he left his sniveling brat of a brother John in charge. The bas—" He stopped, giving Maryam a sideways look. "Let's just say he's never met a tax he wouldn't raise. He declared a 'state of emergency' to support the war, and he's levied taxes on nearly every merchant, farmer and tradesman in the entire kingdom. No one can pay what he demands. And you can't charge more to shoe a horse to cover the tax because no one else has money to pay you either." He kicked at a log in the fire and sparks rose. The sun was peeking over the eastern sky, but it was still dark and overcast, and the flaming flecks swirled up into the air like swarms of bees.

"I'm sorry," I said.

He shrugged his giant shoulders. "I couldn't keep my smithy open, and one day a group of King's Guards showed up with the Shire Reeve. John was sending his own guards out to collect taxes. I guess the bailiffs and the reeves couldn't collect it fast enough to feed his little pig face. Anyway, they told me what I owed and knew I couldn't pay it. So they took my equipment and things got rough. I took on six of them, and gave 'em a licking, that's for certain," he said.

"Maybe I'm beginning to like you after all," Robard muttered.

John laughed. "Wasn't anything left for me there. They tried dragging me off for assault, but I broke loose, took a horse and ran. I've been hiding out here ever since. When I served with Sir Thomas in King Henry's army, I learned to always make sure I had a backup plan. Always kept a cache of tools and a few crosslets hidden nearby, enough to make do for a while. I found that bridge there and have been charging a toll to whoever passes by. I expect some baron owns the land, and he'll find me out soon enough and I'll have to move on. It's thievin', what I'm doing, I guess, but what else can a man do?"

We each nodded, not knowing what to tell him. The pottage bubbled on the fire and smelled delicious, and John passed out a wooden plate that we shared, eating until we had our fill. Robard sat down next to Maryam and filled the plate, letting her eat first before he took his meal. When he was finished, he scooped out a bit and blew on it to cool, placing it on the ground for Angel. She devoured it in three gulps, then curled up by the fire and went instantly to sleep.

"What are your plans now, Tristan? Why did Sir Thomas order you away from his side?" Little John asked.

"I have very important dispatches for the Master of the Order. Sir Thomas ordered me to deliver them to . . . London . . . but I . . . ah . . . learned . . . the Master is in Scotland. So I must travel there to find him. I met Robard and Maryam along the way and we've been traveling together ever since." I hadn't lied, much, but I had withheld most of the truth. Desperately wanting to steer the conversation away from Sir Thomas and my duty, I asked, "What are you going to do, John?"

He was quiet for a moment as he stared into the fire. "I'm not certain. I really haven't thought about it. I keep hoping some of the nobles will rise up and knock some sense into Prince John, but we could easily starve before that happens."

"I have an idea. There is a place, not far from here, where you might be useful. Why don't you travel with us? If I'm not completely lost, it's only a day's ride. If it doesn't work out, you can always return here and reopen your toll bridge."

Robard sat up straight as I finished, and even Maryam's eyes were wide. "Tristan! A word, please!" Robard said as he grabbed me by the arm, pulling me some distance from the fire. If Little John took notice of Robard's actions, he pretended not to.

"What in the world are you thinking?" Robard asked.

"About what?" I said nonchalantly.

"No games, Tristan, you understand very well what!" Robard whispered.

"Robard, as you and Maryam so recently pointed out to me, we are in a fight for our lives. You have *met* Little John, have you not? Don't you think having someone like him on our side would be an asset?"

"He's big, I'll give you that. And . . . deceptively fast. But how well do you know this man? He made your sword? You talked to him for a few minutes several months ago? It's not much to base a friendship on. Besides, I don't like him."

"Well, there's no surprise there. Did I tell you he saved my hide once? And Sir Thomas himself swore to his character? Besides, I based our entire friendship on the fact that you came to my aid when those bandits attacked me in Outremer," I countered.

"This isn't about me—of course *I'm* trustworthy. So what if he did save you from the King's Guards? You see how he's been living. He's turned to thievery. Why—"

"What story did you tell me when we first met?" I interrupted. "Of the man you knew back home who killed one of the King's deer to feed his starving family? Wouldn't we all turn to thieving if we were hungry enough?"

"Ahh. I don't like this. This is *not* a good idea. Besides, what place are you referring to, a day's ride from here? Where do you want to take him? Surely you don't mean all the way to Scotland?"

"No," I said. "Not Scotland. Tomorrow we're riding straight to St. Alban's. I need to go home."

12

ittle John agreed to ride on with us the next morning. He gathered up his meager belongings in a small cloth bag, which he slung over his shoulder. He left us alone briefly to retrieve his mount, hobbled deep in the woods. Watching him ride turned out to be quite humorous, since he was nearly as big as the horse. He sat low in the saddle, his feet nearly dragging on the ground.

Robard and John worked toward an uneasy peace. They avoided each other for the most part, and whenever we stopped to water and rest the horses, they didn't speak to or acknowledge each other in any way. Maryam and I were more than content to let things go as they were. Angel, however, had fully accepted Little John as a member of our group, and I couldn't deny it felt safer having him along with us.

As we rode toward St. Alban's, I finally had a moment to give more thought to the Queen Mother and her improbable declaration. Sir Hugh had seen us in Dover. He would send word to Eleanor of Aquitaine, and she would certainly send more soldiers to help in the search.

We had encountered no patrols since racing from Dover. We'd skirted every town and village, and succeeded in avoiding any contact with Templars or King's Guards. Assuming they had lost our trail, at least for a while, I allowed myself some small measure of hope. Here, on our home soil, and with the help of my friends, we might actually be able to escape Sir Hugh's clutches.

"You've been very quiet lately," Maryam said to me as we rode along.

"Hmm? Oh, sorry. Just thinking is all," I said, distracted.

"What about?" she asked.

"The usual questions," I said. "Is Sir Hugh following us? Where are the King's Guards? How will we get to Scotland? And I'm wondering if—" I stopped, not wanting to mention Celia's name out loud and be teased relentlessly for it. But I found that as we drew farther away from Sir Hugh and whenever I was not fighting for my life, Celia's face invaded my memory.

Maryam and I trotted easily at the head of our small column. Robard and Little John followed.

"She does, you know," Maryam said after I'd been silent a moment.

"What? Who does?" I asked, confused.

"Celia. She thinks of you, Tristan."

"I didn't . . . I . . . Do you really think so?" I stammered. It was no use to deny that Celia had been what I was thinking about. Maryam just knew these things.

"Of course," she said.

"How do you know?" I asked her.

"By the time we left Montségur, Celia was already in love with you. Of course you didn't know it."

90

"What? Don't be ridiculous. We hardly even talked or . . . We barely know each other," I protested.

"You don't choose love, Tristan, love chooses you. Think of it. You went back to help her. At great cost and sacrifice, I might add. Don't you remember how she looked at you when we entered the gates of her fortress?" she asked. "When she saw you there, the happiness in her eyes . . . Trust me, it was love." In truth I had no idea how she had looked at me, for I could only remember being awestruck by seeing her there again.

"Looked at me? What . . . I . . . don't . . . Maryam, that's crazy," I said.

"It might be, but it's also true," she said. She goaded her horse forward and rode ahead of me, as if to say that in her opinion, the matter was closed.

Toward the afternoon, we had to stop more frequently as John's horse struggled to keep up with us under the immense girth of its rider. I kept my voice low, for I had no wish for Robard, or especially Little John, to overhear. When we were besieged at Montségur, I had told my friends the true nature of the task Sir Thomas had lain before me, and Maryam had readily embraced it as the truth, informing us she had heard the song of the Grail in Outremer. Robard still didn't believe I carried the Holy Grail. And as much as I trusted that Little John was noble and good, I did not intend to reveal to him the full extent of my mission.

We spent an hour in the late morning stopping to rest and building a small fire to warm ourselves. My wound ached considerably, and I strode back and forth near the fire, trying to work the soreness out of it. Maryam could see I was still troubled and approached me while Robard and Little John squatted by the fire, eyeing each other like two dogs measuring the distance to the last bone, each one waiting for the other to pounce first. Angel sat between them, watching them with curiosity.

"How are you feeling?" she asked.

"Much better. Stronger every day, in fact," I said. In truth riding horseback was growing unbearable. But remaining in one place long enough to heal was not an option.

"That's not what I meant," she said. "Is something on your mind besides the fair Celia?"

I shrugged. Maryam had an uncanny ability to extract information from me. She could read my moods and somehow found a way to make me reveal my secrets, often before I even realized what I was saying. And if my answers became short and clipped, she probed harder until she had sniffed out the truth. She'd never admit it, of course. Part of her wanted *me* to believe she couldn't tell when I withheld things from her. But she was always a step or three ahead of me.

"Something has been bothering you ever since we escaped the castle in Calais. What is it?" She went straight to the point.

"Really, it's just my wound. Getting shot is no small thing. A seeping wound in one's side tends to cut down on happy thoughts, you know."

"Yes," she said, flexing the very shoulder Robard's arrow had wounded in Outremer. "But it's not the wound, it's something else. You act puzzled."

"Hmm. Well, you could be right. I'm trying to figure out a way to keep us all from getting captured and thrown into prison. Or worse. I'd almost rather have Sir Hugh right in front of me, because at least then I'd know where he was. Having him in the shadows makes me jumpy. And as you both so recently reminded me, the only way out of this is for us, or rather me, to kill him. I, a squire to a Templar Knight, must somehow defeat a Marshal of the Order if he doesn't slay me first."

"Robard or I would be more than happy to dispatch him for you," she said. A small smile came over her face at the thought of killing Sir Hugh.

"I appreciate it. Really, I do. But somehow, I think it must fall to me."

"Almost since the moment I met you, Sir Hugh has been chasing you . . . us." She glanced over her shoulder to the fire, making sure Little John was out of earshot. "And it's not the Grail that's troubling you. We could easily see your relief when you revealed your secret to us. But ever since the castle, upon encountering that horrible queen . . ." Her voice trailed off.

"All right. I'll tell you what happened. But it has to be some kind of trick or deception Eleanor and Sir Hugh have concocted to distract me. I'm sure there is nothing to it. When we . . . and you were . . . on the barrel, just as Sir Hugh was about to . . . ," I stammered, not wanting to relive it. "Eleanor said something to me."

"Men!" Maryam sighed quietly. "Will you get on with it? What?! She told you what, Tristan?!"

"Eleanor . . . She said she would see me dead before I ever sat on Richard's throne."

Maryam's black eyes flew open in amazement.

"What!?" she whispered.

"What?" Robard interjected from behind us, never taking his eyes off Little John.

"Nothing!" we both said at once.

We stood silently for a while as Maryam considered my revelation.

"Do you suppose she was serious?" she finally asked.

"I don't know. One moment she appeared quite sane. The next moment she was cackling away like a crazy witch," I said.

"What are you two mumbling about over there?" Robard asked again.

"It's nothing, really, Robard. Tristan just thought he might have seen something in the woods is all," Maryam said.

"What? Where? Was it Templars? Guards? It could be bandits!" He leapt to his feet, his head swiveling back and forth, scanning the trail ahead of us for any sign of trouble.

"I think I was mistaken," I said, glaring at Maryam. But before she could say anything else, we mounted up again and rode off.

Robard rode beside us for a long while, giving us little chance to talk further. I wasn't ready to tell him yet. He undoubtedly would not believe me, and would make jokes I was not in the mood for.

After midday, we found the traveler's road. Although seeing something so familiar was thrilling, I was hesitant to take such a well-used thoroughfare. But I worried we might become lost and not find St. Alban's otherwise. And as the day rolled along, the woods and forest became more recognizable to me. We were getting closer. The weather was turning colder, and I welcomed the thought of a warm fire and delicious meal waiting for us at the abbey.

We finally broke through the forest and there before us was the abbey gate. I was so excited I gave rein to my horse and dashed up the lane leading to the courtyard, with my friends following quickly behind me. It took me a moment to realize something was wrong.

The trail leading to the abbey was lined with wooden crosses, each pushed carefully into the ground. None of them had been there when I'd left. I pulled my horse to a stop and jumped down, examining each one. From one cross hung a brother's robe. Another held the abbot's rosary. I would know it anywhere, for I'd seen it every day of my life, hanging from the rope belt he cinched around his waist. Each cross held a similar marker. Brother Rupert's sandals. On another was a small crucifix that had belonged to Brother Christian, who had joined the order just a few short years ago. What was this? This couldn't be. All of them? Buried here beneath the trees?

My heart rose in my throat, and I hurried back into my saddle as best my wound would allow and rode hard up the lane to the abbey courtyard. More crosses marked the way. First four, then ten, then twenty. Dear God, what had happened? Please, I prayed. Don't let this be! It must have been some sickness. A plague must have struck a local village and the sick had come here seeking comfort in their dying days and had been buried along the lane. Please don't let it be the brothers.

But the momentary joy I'd felt at the thought of being home turned immediately to anguish as I arrived in the courtyard and saw what lay before me.

"No!" I cried. I leapt from my horse and dropped to my knees, unable to hold back the tears. "NO!"

St. Alban's Abbey had been burned to the ground.

13

y former home was a skeleton of ashes and cinders. The fire had been efficient: only a few charred timbers remained upright. In my soul, I knew it was the work of Sir Hugh. In Tyre, while he'd held us in our jail cells, he had sneered while telling me he had tortured the monks. I assumed then that he was bluffing, trying to scare me into revealing the location of the Grail to him. But it was no bluff. On my first night with the regimento in Dover, I remembered seeing him talking with two King's Guards outside the Commandery. They had been secretive and cunning in their movements, and the guards had left him, riding off to the west. They must have come here. Why? If only I had told Sir Thomas! He might have been able to save them.

Sobs wracked my body. This was my fault. If I had refused Sir Thomas' offer to join the Templars, if I had stayed here, none of this would have happened. Nothing made sense.

Maryam put her arm gently around my shoulders. "Tristan . . . ," she said quietly.

"No . . . no . . . no . . . ," I moaned, pounding the ground in frustration. "He killed them. He killed them all."

Robard knelt down, also putting his arm on my shoulder. "Come, Tristan," he said softly, trying vainly to pull me to my feet. "We'll find out what happened here, I promise—"

"No!" I shouted, skittering away from them. "Don't you see? He killed them all! They were completely innocent and he burned them to death! And it's my fault!"

"Lad," Little John spoke. "Who is it you speak of? I knew of this abbey. If it burned by treachery, who would do such a foul thing?"

But I couldn't say anything more. I lay there on the ground, folded up like a turtle in its shell, rocking back and forth.

"Tristan," Robard said. "Those graves we found, we don't know who lies in them. And perhaps the fire was an accident. . . . If Sir Hugh—"

"Sir Hugh?" Little John interrupted. "Sir Hugh Montfort? Of Sir Thomas' regimento? Is he the one you refer to?"

"It is," Robard replied. "Why do you ask?"

"I've run afoul of him many times. When Thomas and I served in the King's Army, he was a minister to the court of King Henry. More crooked than a thistle's root, he is. What does he have to do with this, Tristan?"

Maryam stood, taking Little John by the arm and walking him a few steps away. She spoke to him in low tones, but I neither heard nor cared what she relayed to him. I stayed on the ground and refused to move. My soul was empty. The only family I had ever known had been destroyed.

"Tristan, steady now," Robard said. "We don't know anything for certain. Maybe those graves—"

"No! He did this. He killed them. Or he sent the King's Guards to do it. Because of me, because that witch Eleanor thinks I am a noble! She thinks I want Richard's throne!"

"Oh!" Maryam exclaimed.

Robard stared at me as if I were insane. Which was entirely possible. It took him a long moment to process what I had said.

"Tristan, I'm very sorry for what you have found here. For your loss. But what did you just say?" he asked.

"When we were in Calais, as I held the Queen Mother hostage, she said she would see me dead before I ever sat on Richard's throne. I told her I'm an orphan, but she thinks I'm born of some noble who has claim to the throne. It's the only explanation. And Eleanor has been working with Sir Hugh all along! Someone must have hidden an orphan child somewhere and those two think it's me. Sir Hugh and Eleanor killed them so they wouldn't tell! To keep Richard and their ridiculous kingdom safe! But I'm not a noble, I can't be. . . . I'm just . . ." Sobs came again. I had never felt so alone.

"Tristan, you are upset. . . . I can't imagine how you must be feeling. But you are talking nonsense. You can't believe . . . that woman. . . . The chances of you . . . My God . . ." Robard stopped, unsure of what else to say.

With his giant hand, Little John gently pulled me to my feet. "Lad," he said. And then he stopped a moment, staring hard at me in the advancing twilight. He studied my face as if he were meeting me for the first time. "You do . . ." But his words trailed off.

"What?" Robard asked.

"I . . . thought . . . It's nothing. It's getting dark. We should find a place to camp for the night. We'll sort this out. Tomorrow . . . those graves . . . Well, I won't lie to you, Tristan, a horrible tragedy has been done here to those who lie beneath those crosses. But your friend is right. Tomorrow I can visit some of the nearby villages, try to find out what happened. Maybe some of the brothers survived."

"No!" I said, jerking my arm away from Little John's grasp. "Leave me be."

I ran, sprinting around the remains of the abbey. At first I heard someone coming after me: Robard. But Maryam called for him to stop.

I ran behind the crumbled pile of rubble and ash to the grounds beyond St. Alban's. The outbuildings and stables were burned as well. So I kept running, not stopping until I passed across the wheat fields and reached the distant woods. With each step, my wounded side caused me to nearly howl in agony, but I wanted the pain. I wanted it to squeeze and encircle me in a red hot rage. I cried as I moved through the trees, dodging limbs and branches and rocks and roots. The faces of the monks appeared everywhere as I ran. The abbot. Brother Rupert. Brother Tuck. What horrors they must have felt at the hands of such evil men.

Finally, I could run no more. There was nothing left inside of me. It was late in the afternoon and the shadows lengthened in the woods. It would be dusk soon. I staggered to a small clearing and slumped against the base of a tree. Resting my back against it, I sat there, arms on my knees, silent tears flowing down my face. There was nothing I could do to bring my friends back. I put my head on my knees and closed my eyes, sobbing until I could cry no more.

I must have dozed, for when I lifted my head, it was dark and the evening woods awakened as the night birds sang. It was getting colder, but the wind and weather did not concern me. The breeze picked up, and the trees swayed as their limbs creaked and knocked against each other.

I peered up at the sky, wanting to curse God for allowing this to happen. I had lost everything. The monks. Sir Thomas. Quincy and Sir Basil. My heart leapt at the thought of Celia. What if Sir Hugh had done the same to her? Let Sir Hugh find me, I thought, for when he did, I would strangle him with my bare hands.

Some instinct brought me back to the present moment—I don't know whether it was the long months of battle or merely an inborn desire for survival, but I sensed movement in the underbrush behind me. Someone or something was attempting a stealthy approach. The evening stars were rising in the sky and there was a dim light to the forest. I listened hard. If my friends had come to retrieve me, I would run away again. I wished only to be left alone.

Another rustle in the bushes convinced me it was no animal. Whoever was there was big, and thus it could not be Maryam or Robard, both of whom would likely be upon me before I even knew either of them was there. It must be Little John, come to find me.

"Who's there?" I demanded. No answer. "Go away!"

There was silence for a moment, but then came the shuffle of footsteps, creeping as quietly as they were able, along the forest floor.

"Leave me alone!" I shouted. My words echoed off the trees, and startled ravens and starlings cried out as they burst into flight.

The woods were stilled momentarily, and the sound resumed. With a heavy sigh I stood up, drawing my sword as I did so.

"Don't come any closer!" I commanded.

Pushing myself out from the tree trunk, I turned to face whoever it was who dared disturb me. "I warned—" I stopped, the words dying in my throat.

For there before me, his gentle face outlined in the starlight, arms open wide, stood someone I knew in an instant. I threw my sword to the ground, staggering forward.

And I fainted dead away into the arms of Brother Tuck.

14

woke to the hum of voices and, opening my eyes, found myself next to a crackling fire. My dreams haunted me, and for a moment I wondered if I still slept. I hoped so. Then all I had learned this day would be part of a horrible, horrible nightmare.

Maryam said, "There you are," and I felt a large warm hand on my forehead, gazing up to see the smiling face of Brother Tuck. It was not a dream. He was really here.

I stood up and so did he, clapping his hands with glee. From the time I was a child, I don't think I've ever seen such an expression of happiness cross his face. His giant hands cradled my head, and he pushed the hair out of my eyes, looking at me like he couldn't believe his luck.

"It's so good to see you," I said. He couldn't hear me, as he was deaf as well as mute, but I touched my heart and pointed at him. Through the years Tuck and I had found our own way of communicating with each other. Using simple signs and motions, I could make him understand what I needed, wanted or sometimes even wished. The abbot once told me Tuck was a genius at "understanding people." Because he could not hear or speak, he had learned to watch our eyes and faces. Even by the way we stood or gestured he could on some level understand what we required of him. Since Tuck had practically raised me, we had our own method of wordless communication, and it surprised me how easily I fell back into it. My heart was overjoyed at finding him alive.

"Everyone, this is Brother Tuck, the monk most responsible for raising me. In fact, it was he who found me on the abbey steps when I was left there as a babe. He is one of the kindest, most decent men I've ever known."

All of them stood and shook hands with Brother Tuck. He watched me carefully as I pointed to each of them and touched my chest near my heart. This told him these three were my friends, and it was all he needed. He would never learn or speak their names, but I had just vouched for them in Tuck's eyes, and that was good enough for him.

Finding St. Alban's in ruins and then discovering Tuck alive had been an enormous shock. Standing by the fire, it took me a moment to get my bearings. We were camped in the woods near the abbey. The campsite was littered with flame-scarred benches, jars, tools and crocks of Tuck's potions and numerous other objects he must have scavenged from the wreckage of St. Alban's.

"Your monk, he cannot speak?" Robard asked. "This is Tuck? The one you've told us stories of?"

I nodded. "Yes, he is deaf and dumb. But he understands things. I guess over the years we developed our own way of 'talking.' I can't explain it. When I was growing up, he was always able to figure out whatever it was I required."

"He carried you back to us," Little John said quietly. The thought of it made me smile for just an instant; to know Tuck was still alive and taking care of me helped lessen my grief. "Then he brought us here. He must have been living in the woods since . . ." He didn't finish his thought. "The poor soul. He probably had no idea what else to do."

"I wish he could tell us what happened," I said. A small portion of a charred bench from the abbey lay not far away. I held it out to Tuck, pointing at the burn marks along the side. "What happened, Tuck? Who did this? Who burned St. Alban's?" I hadn't believed Sir Hugh back in Tyre, but now I knew in my mind and heart that he was responsible. If only Tuck could confirm it.

Moving past me, he went to a fallen log that lay just outside the circle of the fire. The log's end was hollow, and from inside it he removed a square metal box, eagerly handing it to me. Removing the lid, I discovered two pieces of parchment inside, one of them wrapped with a small ribbon.

I unwound the ribbon and, kneeling by the fire, found the page covered in the abbot's neat, precise handwriting. The sight of it, so familiar, made me choke back tears.

Dear Tristan,

Praise our heavenly Father. I have made Brother Tuck understand he should give this box to you and you alone. I have prayed to God you will return here someday, and if you are reading this, it must mean he has once again answered my prayers. As when you landed upon our steps those many years ago, Tuck is another miracle God has sent to us. Our abbey has been blessed by both of you. God is truly great in his generosity in bringing two such fine men to our home.

If you are reading this letter, however, I am no longer alive. With prayer and the grace of God, I have lived long enough to leave you my last words.

But first, I beg you as a good Christian to promise you will not seek revenge on those who have done us this terrible harm. The Bible commands us to forgive them and pray for them. These are words we have lived our life by: compassion and forgiveness. And we must not abandon them now. Vengeance belongs to the Lord our Father, not mortal man. And seeking the same would only poison your heart and soul. Promise me this, as my last dying wish.

What you hold in your hands will tell you much but not everything. Not long after you left with Sir Thomas and the Templars, men came here in the night. They questioned us brutally. But they learned nothing. We protected you as a babe and we protect you unto death. Sir Thomas will decide when you must learn the answers you seek.

It is God's blessing Tuck was not here when the King's Guards came for us. When we refused to answer their questions, God forgive them but they locked us inside and set fire to the abbey. They guarded the doors and windows so we could not escape. May God have mercy on their souls. Somehow I survived my injuries long enough for Tuck to find me. He has treated me with his potions and herbs, but God tells me my time is near.

I do not know why you have returned to St. Alban's, but I promise you, your secret dies with me. It is for your own safety.

Hold the memory of your brothers here in your heart. Mourn

for them, but do not despair, for they now reside with our Father in
Heaven. You need only live on. Follow your heart and be kind and true
to what we have taught you, Tristan, and their deaths will not have
been in vain.

Go in peace.

Abbot Geoffrey Reneau.
St. Alban's. March 1191.

Along with the abbot's letter were two other pieces of parchment.
The first was a proclamation:

By Royal Order of Her Majesty the Queen
REWARD
The Queen seeks the whereabouts of a male child.
Likely left at a nunnery or monastery or with a peasant family.
Crosslets 500 for information leading to his whereabouts.
Crosslets 1,000 if the child is delivered alive to Gloucester Castle.
Do not attempt deception. It will be dealt with in
the most severe manner.
Royal seal affixed this date, 1174,
August High Counsel to Her Majesty the Queen,
Eleanor of Aquitaine,
Hugh St. Montfort

In the flickering firelight I read the final sheet. It was brief, only a
few lines. But affixed to the top of the page was the royal seal of
Henry II. It read:

Father Geoffrey;

I pray the boy is now safe. Watch over him. I trust you to determine when he is ready to know the truth. When you feel the time is right, send him to me, but his safety must be paramount.

I will send travelers to the abbey now and then to keep watch. You won't know who they are and neither will he.

Your service in this matter will not go unrewarded.

With my sincerest thanks,

Henry II,
Sovereign of England

The handwriting on the last sheet was instantly familiar to me. Inside my satchel I kept the note that had been left with me on the steps of St. Alban's. With shaking hands, I unwrapped the oilskin I'd kept it in for these long months. I placed it next to the note signed by Henry II, the Lionheart's father and once the King of England.

They were identical.

15

hat do the papers say?" Robard asked.

"They say . . ." But I couldn't finish. Staggering to the fire, I sat down on one of the benches Brother Tuck had plucked from the ashes of the abbey.

"Tristan." Maryam left her seat, kneeling in front of me. "Tristan, I am your friend and would gladly give everything I have not to see you in such pain. But we are here with you and there is nothing you can tell us, nothing written on any piece of paper, that would change anything. We are with you, now and always."

"Maryam . . . it says . . . It's from the abbot. A letter . . . There is a note here from King Henry. . . ." I could barely speak. What I'd wished to learn my entire life was tantalizingly close. The abbot knew. I wasn't an orphan. He knew all along. He and Sir Thomas were in this together. Had Sir Thomas deceived me? Was making me his squire part of a larger plot?

As he had done ever since I could remember, Brother Tuck rushed to my side to brush the tears away. But they would not stop, and his face grew concerned. According to the abbot's letter it was only because of luck that Tuck had not been here when the King's

Guards arrived, but he had still witnessed something horrible happen to his home. And though he might never fully understand the details, he recognized the source of my grief.

Handing the parchments to Maryam, I buried my head in my hands, more confused than ever. The abbot and the brothers had died keeping my secret from Sir Hugh. Sir Thomas was meant to explain everything to me when the "time was right," but no one could have expected Sir Thomas to die fighting in Acre. Now I had nothing.

"Oh," Maryam exclaimed as she read the pages. She looked at me with eyes wide. "Tristan, this letter from King Henry, the handwriting . . . Did you notice?"

"Notice what? What!?" Robard said impatiently.

"The note Tristan has carried forever, the one left with him here . . . when he was orphaned—it was written by King Henry," she said.

Little John let out a low whistle. "Tristan, lad . . . what does this mean?" he asked.

"Nothing. It doesn't mean anything. Just because King Henry may have written some note, that doesn't mean anything," I said. My head was fuzzy and full of mush. From where she was lying on the ground by the fire, Angel padded over and sniffed at my face, licking my cheek before she curled up into a ball at my side.

"Tristan," Maryam said, "could it be that . . . You said Eleanor believed you were born of a noble. Could it be your King Henry is . . . was . . . ?" She stumbled over the words, her faced knitted in deep thought. "This makes it sound like he was your father!" Little John and Robard gasped.

"I thought you . . . ," Little John said slowly. Then he waved his hand in the air, as if pushing the words away.

My mind was too full to consider it. These letters explained a great deal. In his mind, the abbot had deceived me for my own safety. But he would not have made up such a tale. Though stern, he was not a cruel man. He would not have told an elaborate lie to me about my parenthood. If I accepted these documents as the truth, it forced me to confront matters I had no energy to deal with. No, it was better for me to go on as I always had. Not knowing who I was.

Maryam came quickly toward me, grasping me by the elbow. I wanted to yank my arm free but she held it too strongly. "Sir Hugh and Eleanor were searching for you . . . when you were first born. . . . This must mean—"

Shrugging my bedroll off my shoulders, I stalked away from the firelight. The loss I felt was too much to bear. Everyone from my childhood was dead. There was no home left for me. And now a massive weight crushed me. I had just been told the one thing I had wanted to know my entire life, and I wished I could take it back. If I'd never met Sir Thomas, none of these horrible things would have happened. They had died because of me. Because someone believed I was a person I couldn't possibly be.

I paced about the camp for several minutes, stalking back and forth. Tuck studied me with a worried expression, but the others said nothing. When I had tired myself out, I lay again by the fire. I made a sleeping motion with my hands, and Tuck smiled and readied his own spot by the fire. As I drifted off to sleep, I could hear Robard and the others talking in low tones. Tuck came and sat cross-legged on the ground next to me, resting his hand on my shoulder. He had lost as much as I had, if not more, and I knew I should offer him comfort. My heart nearly cleaved in two at the thought of poor Tuck returning to the abbey to find it either in flames or ashes. In between caring for the abbot he must have dug each grave and prayed for the departed souls of his brothers. I was certain it was he who had marked each cross with a memento. I could not bear the thought of it, that my own foolish existence had brought death and destruction down upon his home.

I drifted into a fitful sleep and woke up more than once calling out for the abbot and Sir Thomas. Several times I opened my eyes to find Maryam or Tuck kneeling beside me, gently attempting to soothe me from my nightmares. When I finally woke before sunup the next morning, my wound still ached, and my head felt like it was full of sheared wool. My mind was empty and reluctant to think anymore. Tuck was squatting by the fire, stirring something in a large pot that smelled delicious. Though I was groggy and disoriented, my mouth watered. I needed to use the tree for enough support to rise, and I couldn't rid myself of the aches and stiffness ravaging my body. As I took a step toward the fire, pain radiated from the wound in my side, and down my leg. I winced and dropped to one knee.

Tuck was there in a heartbeat. He pushed the hair back from my eyes, feeling my face for heat. He pulled my hand away from where it clasped my side, and we were both shocked to find blood on my hand. His eyes widened and he hurried away, returning in a short time with a small crock full of one of his potions.

I never knew what Tuck put in his peculiar mixtures. But I was not worried as he cut away my shirt, clearing space around the wound. He had studied all the plants and wildlife of the forest, and experimented with dozens of different concoctions for healing and soothing. From the jar he applied a greenish, rather foul-smelling paste to my injury.

My howls woke everyone in the camp. Robard and Maryam were so shocked that they immediately assumed we were under attack. "Whaaa!" Robard yelled as he sprang from the ground.

Whatever Tuck had given me, it made my eyes burn and water, and I prayed for relief. For a moment, I wondered if he'd somehow inserted a large wasp inside the wound. The paste felt as if it were burning through my flesh.

"It's nothing." I grimaced. "Just one of Tuck's salves. But, oh, it burns!"

Maryam returned her daggers to their sheaths and harrumphed at me. "Don't whine. Being shot by a longbow hurts much worse."

"No it doesn't," I said.

Slowly the pain from Tuck's concoction receded, and the bleeding stopped. But my mood did not improve. As everyone finished their breakfast, I sat apart, stewing in my own grief and feeling disconnected from the world around me.

Several times Maryam or one of the others tried to draw me into conversation, but I would snap at them and turn away. Even in my funk, I watched Maryam and Robard share a wooden plate of food. As we had traveled these past few weeks, whenever we built a fire, they would sit next to each other. Whatever food we'd managed to hunt or find, Robard would always wait until Maryam had eaten her fill, no matter how hungry he was. After we had escaped Montségur and traveled through France for many weeks, Robard had done all of the hunting and most of the cooking. We would have starved if not for him. He delighted in cooking whatever game he found and serving it to Maryam. And I could tell she appreciated it. Most of the time their growing closeness made me happy. Today it only annoyed me.

Finally, after I had snarled and snapped, and had offended each of them in some way, Robard challenged me directly.

"What's next, Tristan? Where do we go from here? What are you going to do now? You have a duty to your knight, don't you?" he asked, intruding on my self-pity.

"Just leave me alone," I said. "I don't know. None if it matters. No matter what we do, death and destruction will follow in our wake." I sat picking at the food Tuck had insisted I take.

"Well, too bloody bad. You need to get ahold of yourself. You've suffered a loss, there's no denying it. More than anyone should have to. But you've got work to do, so I say let's get to it."

"No. Don't you realize what's happened here? You don't—" I stammered.

Robard grabbed me by the shirt and pulled me to my feet, his face inches from mine. "Enough of this, Tristan. We're sorry for what happened here, but we will grieve for your friends in time. Have you forgotten Sir Hugh is still looking for us? And the King's Guards? And Eleanor won't stop either. Don't you think it might occur to them that you might come here? Looking for a place to rest or hide? Sir Hugh is probably on his way here now. You made an oath to your knight. You have a duty. If you sit around here feeling sorry for yourself, you're going to get us killed," he said.

I tried to push away, but Robard's grip was like iron. Angel let out a low growl and Brother Tuck moved toward us, worried Robard might try to hurt me. Little John held out his hand and gently pulled Tuck back.

"You don't understand! These men died . . ." I tried not to cry again, but the tears wouldn't stop.

"You think you're the only one who's suffered in this world? Are you the only one to lose a friend or comrade? You've had a tough road, Tristan, I'll grant you, but you need to be strong now. Let's finish this."

I wanted to do what Robard said. Last night I had wanted to hunt Sir Hugh down. But this morning, I'd awakened drained and empty with no more stomach for it. I just wanted to be left to die amidst the ruins of my beloved home.

My head sagged and Robard sighed. He let go of me and I slumped to the ground again. He stomped away.

"Maryam, let's get the horses ready. Little John . . . tell me, don't you find it odd that someone your size is called Little John? I do. It's not the best nickname I've ever heard. Maybe I should call you Tiny instead." Robard paused a moment, as if considering it. "Regardless, Little John, I'm not sure you're to be trusted, but you may come with us as well if you'd like. We leave in ten minutes," Robard commanded, pulling me to my feet again and pushing me toward the horses. "Figure out a way to get your Brother Tuck to gather up what he needs, because we're leaving."

"What? No. What are you doing?" I complained.

"I'm taking you somewhere you can rest and recover and get your mind focused again on what it is you need to do. Lucky for you it's on the way to Scotland," he said.

"Why are you doing this? Where are you taking me?" I groaned.

"I'm taking you home," Robard replied with a smile. "Sherwood Forest."

here were five of us now and only three mounts. While Robard and Maryam prepared the horses for departure, Tuck disappeared. None of us even noticed he was gone until I heard the clicking sound he often made when he was working or thinking or happy. It was a soft noise he made with his tongue, and over the years I'd learned what he meant by the different clicks he could make.

When I glanced around, my heart caught in my throat, for there stood Tuck, with our old plow horse Charlemagne at his side. The very horse the brothers lent me to ride to Dover when I left St. Alban's with the knights. I had no idea how Tuck had recovered Charlemagne, but seeing him was a momentary lift of my spirits. Rushing to Charlemagne's side, I smiled as he nickered in recognition and pushed his head against my chest.

Maryam and Robard again shared a horse. Tuck tied up a few cloth bags and looped them over Charlemagne's back, then mounted up, and we took our leave of St. Alban's. I removed the documents from the abbot's box and placed them in my satchel. I still did not wish to leave, but in the end there was no choice.

Robard was determined he would take me with him one way or the other. I couldn't summon the energy to argue with him, so I reluctantly followed along.

We rode back through the woods to the abbey grounds, and I asked my companions for a few moments to pray at the graves of my brothers. Tuck joined me, and there were tears in his eyes as we knelt there. As a child, I often wondered how Tuck knew how and when to pray. I once asked the abbot, and he told me he believed God spoke directly to special souls like Tuck and that Tuck had no need of human speech or hearing. Perhaps he was right, but as we knelt in the lane and prayed for the souls of the monks, I gave thanks. As angry as I was at God, he had also created a miracle in his kind and gentle servant Brother Tuck.

We headed north, and Robard, Maryam and the others left me alone as we traveled through the countryside. Even Angel kept her distance, but she found another friend, as she clearly delighted in Brother Tuck's company. We rode during the day, avoiding farms and villages. On occasion Robard doubled back to make sure we weren't being followed.

Winter fully arrived a few days later, and the weather, which had been cool, grew colder. Tuck replaced my lost tunic with a brown monk's robe from one of his bags and insisted I wear it. The thick wool helped to cut some of the wind and cold, but I worried the weather would slow us up. We needed to make fires at night or risk freezing, which worked in Sir Hugh's favor, as they made us easier to find.

The leaves had fallen from trees and everything around us was gray and barren. On occasion snowflakes swirled through the sky. We slept close to the fire at night.

When I tried to sleep, I was haunted by the faces of the brothers. They tormented me and I continued blaming myself for their deaths. I thought of Eleanor's proclamation in Calais, and of Sir Thomas. The abbot had deceived me all these years. He knew who I was, but had kept it from me so I would be safe. But now Sir Thomas was dead, and the full truth of my parentage had died with him. Death followed me everywhere, and in my darkest moments of despair, I cursed God. If he hadn't seen fit to guide me to St. Alban's, the brothers would still be alive.

As we moved farther north, Robard's spirits improved with each passing day. He was happy to be going home, something he had yearned for since I first met him in Outremer. And despite my foul mood, I tried to be happy for him. He took special pride in showing Maryam the many things he knew about the forest.

Yet try as I might, I could not lift the veil of darkness overwhelming me. When we camped at night, I would often stalk off into the woods alone to practice with my sword, swinging it back and forth, thrusting and parrying until, despite the cold weather, the sweat dripped from my brow. Maryam and even Tuck in his own silent way would beg me to rest. But I refused. My wounded side ached, but Tuck kept applying his poultices, and eventually it stopped hurting as much.

We circled around London, staying closer to the coast, and found a spot where we could swim the horses across the Thames. The water was dreadfully cold, and once across we needed to stop and build a fire immediately to warm ourselves before turning back inland and heading toward Robard's homestead. We passed a few cities and towns on the way, Northampton and Leicester and other places I knew of only from the tales of travelers who had visited St. Alban's.

But trouble was following us. I felt it, and I think the others did too. In France, while I had gone to Celia's aid, I had felt a presence lurking behind me and knew it was Sir Hugh. I wondered if somehow it was the Grail warning me.

Two days past the Thames, Robard rode hurriedly into the small glen where we were resting the horses.

"Templars!" he said. "Quickly." We all leapt to the saddle and hurried off. Three leagues away, we found a spot offering good cover on a ridge above a well-traveled road. Dismounting, we hid in the trees and waited. A few minutes later a dozen Templars thundered by below us. Sir Hugh was not among them, but they were going hard, pushing their horses. We waited until they were well past before we started out again. It was a close call, and if Robard hadn't been watching, they likely would have ridden right upon us. I couldn't tell if they were Sir Hugh's men or not, but I now assumed every commandery in England was on the lookout. In my darker moments I believed Sir Hugh was the devil himself, and seeing these men only served to remind me that his fingers were in every corner of the kingdom.

We became more cautious. It was impossible to travel without being seen occasionally, and Sir Hugh had proven before to be an able tracker. No matter our pace, where we camped or how cautiously we proceeded, someone was going to notice us.

After many more days, we passed around a village that Robard called Loughborough.

"We're close, my friends," he exclaimed happily. "We're no more than a good day's journey from my family's farm now. We'll find shelter there and plenty of food. We can safely rest while we plan our next move."

Seven days had passed since we'd left St. Alban's. Mostly we traveled in the early morning and at twilight, resting in the middle of the day when more people were about and the likelihood of being discovered was higher. Riding at night had finally proved too difficult. We became lost on more than one occasion, and unless we followed a well-used road, we made poor time picking our way through the wooded countryside.

While we camped at night, Little John told me stories of Sir Thomas and the time they spent together in King Henry's army, in an effort to lift my spirits. Since the incident on the bridge, Robard took to insulting John whenever he could. This night, Robard scoffed at his story. "From listening to you talk, it would appear that you and Sir Thomas defeated the French single-handedly. Good thing it was only the French and not Saracens." Little John bristled but let the comment slide. In these passing days I learned he was far more patient than Robard, and the rest of us found we enjoyed his company. He took a special interest in Tuck, letting the monk use his potions and creams to treat a variety of ailments I suspected did not really exist. But it made Tuck feel useful.

Whenever Robard tried to draw him into an argument, he would control his temper, and it really annoyed Robard that he was so slow to anger. One morning, as we were readying to break camp, they nearly came to blows. Little John was again telling me stories of his army service under King Henry and some of the details of his campaigns with Sir Thomas. I loved hearing his tales, especially about Sir Thomas. After one particularly adventuresome account of their defeat of French knights, Robard couldn't resist.

"Ha. It sounds like you won the war single-handedly. From your description it sounds as if the French folded like a tent in a windstorm . . . ," he remarked as he was mounting his horse. Robard didn't get the chance to finish. Little John flew across the campsite and pulled Robard off the horse with one hand, tossing him to the ground and knocking the breath from his lungs.

Maryam moved to intercede and I put out an arm to stop her. "Wait," I said quietly.

Little John stood squatting over Robard, who tried to regain his feet but was held effortlessly on the forest floor by the giant man. "Listen to me, archer, and hear me well. You are a soldier and a man of honor, and I do not dispute it. You've spoken of your father and his father, who have also defended the kingdom, and their sacrifice is noted. The Hode family has my gratitude. But know this: you are not the only man who has served. You are not the only Crusader who has seen the waste of lives and terror of warfare. I won't tolerate rude behavior, especially when it comes to my service in the name of England. Are we clear?"

Robard's face reddened as he struggled to free himself. But I saw John's words finally reach him, and his anger subsided. "All right, Little John. I apologize. You are right, I had no call to make light of your service." Little John nodded, and Robard extended his hand and was helped to his feet. Without another word he mounted his horse and rode off, not waiting for us to follow behind him.

As the morning passed, Robard grew more animated. "We're close, my friends. Sherwood lies to the west of Nottingham. We can be there by nightfall if we push hard enough! We'll dine at my father's table and you'll see some of the finest land in all of England." He went on in a similar vein until we were no longer listening.

In the late afternoon, still many hours from Robard's home, according to his estimate, we decided to make camp. The horses could go no farther without rest. Robard argued to keep pushing on, but Little John and Maryam counseled against it.

"Now is not the time to grow careless," Little John cautioned. "Let's say we keep going and find ourselves surrounded by Templars or King's Guards. Our horses are less than fleet as it is. We could not outrun well-mounted troops."

Robard finally agreed. We made our camp in a small stand of trees with a shallow stream nearby. My bones ached from riding, and I welcomed the freedom from the saddle. We ate a dinner of smoked hare and fell fast asleep.

The next morning we woke to find the woods shrouded in fog. It had grown considerably colder overnight, and we wasted no time building a fire. With any luck, Robard told us, we'd be sitting by his hearth come evening.

The mist swirled over and around and through the trees, making it difficult to see more than a few yards in any direction. The forest was quiet, and the birds and other sounds you would expect to hear even on a winter morning were missing. As we gathered up our gear and saddled the horses, Robard paced about the camp nervously.

"Is something wrong?" Little John asked.

"I'm not sure," Robard finally answered.

"Do you think we're in danger?" Maryam asked, her hands unconsciously moving inside the sleeves of her tunic.

"No. Maybe. I don't know. It might just be the weather," he said. "My father used to call a foggy morning like this 'a bandit's day.' It's easier for someone up to no good to move about the forest. I guess it's just . . . nothing, I'm sure."

Everyone hurried to get under way as Robard circled the campsite, peering through the mist and straining to listen to the sounds of the forest. It was just past sunup, but it would be some time before the fog was burned away. He strung his bow before he mounted his horse, and rode with it in his left hand across the pommel of his saddle.

As it turned out, he was right about the weather. It was a perfect day for bandits. Less than half a league from our camp five men stepped out of the fog and demanded that we halt. They were dressed as foresters and like Robard carried longbows, but their faces were hidden by hooded cloaks.

And they each had an arrow nocked and pointed at us.

heir sudden appearance was so shocking that I nearly cried out. After a moment, two of the bandits took the lead horses by the reins while two others blocked our retreat. We were effectively cut off.

Despite our situation, Robard was a study in calm determination, his hands in the air.

"Who are you?" he demanded.

None of them answered. Without speaking, the leader directed the others with a series of shrugs and shakes of his head, the arrow in his bow never wavering from the center of Robard's chest. One of the men went for Sir Thomas' battle sword at Robard's waist. He removed it, belt and all, and slung the sword over his shoulder. I was thankful for the robe Tuck had given me, for I had taken to wearing the satchel beneath it so it was not visible. I strained to listen, hoping for the Grail to sound, assuring me we would survive this encounter, but it was silent.

"You'll answer for this," Robard said. "I know these woods and know them well. There is nowhere you can hide that I won't find you."

His threats had no effect. The thieves stood as still as statues, save for the one gathering up our valuables. Brother Tuck made his familiar clicking sound as the man advanced and rocked back and forth nervously astride his horse. He was scared, and I worried he might do something to cause himself harm.

"Easy, Tuck," I said, reaching over to take him by the arm, hoping I could calm him.

Maryam started acting like a frightened girl. "What do you want with us?" she whined. "Please don't hurt us!" She dropped her reins, slumping in the saddle, and cried the worst fake tears I'd ever heard. But as she hugged her arms, I could see she was reaching up the sleeves of her tunic.

The cowled leader, however, kept his eyes on Robard. Finally, he said quietly, "Drop the bow."

Robard still clutched his bow in one hand. "I think not," he replied.

"I don't want to shoot you, but I will if I have to. Release it."

"Not on your life," Robard answered.

"Drop it! Or it's an arrow for your morning meal!"

The bandit standing next to Tuck was momentarily distracted and thus caught completely unaware when the monk goaded his horse forward and brought his giant fist down on top of the bandit's head. The man crumpled to the ground as if he had been felled by an ax.

"Now!" Robard shouted. I dropped the reins and winced as I rolled backward off my horse. The distinctive twang of a bowstring sounded, and for a moment I swore I felt the rush of air as an arrow passed through the space where I had been just an instant before.

I landed on my feet with my horse between me and the bandit on my right, and drew my sword. Maryam's ululating cry echoed off the trees, and Robard's shouts and curses rang through the morning air. To my left, Little John shouted that he and Tuck had already subdued the other archer. Angel barked and growled and snapped. She was no doubt making life difficult for one of the thieves, but I kept my focus on the man just beyond my horse.

Since they had probably intended to steal our mounts to begin with, and they appeared well trained and organized, I assumed the bandit was too disciplined to shoot one of the horses. Keeping the animal between us, I grabbed its halter and whacked its rump, steering it at a quick pace toward the bandit.

The man was brave, I'll give him that. He held his ground. When I was nearly upon him, I whacked the horse on the rump again and this time he reared, forelegs flashing and kicking while the bandit shouted in alarm.

Twisting and charging around the horse, I was close on the man before he could get a shot off. I swung my sword and he jumped back, holding his bow out in front of him for protection. The flashing steel cut through the wood with little resistance, and it flew apart. Without a second thought, the man turned and ran, disappearing into the foggy woods.

We had nearly triumphed. One man lay on the ground unconscious. Little John held one, his giant arm around the man's neck. Maryam had one pinned to the ground, a golden dagger at his throat.

Only Robard and the leader still grappled. They had both dropped their bows and wrestled hand to hand, trading blows right and left, but neither gained an advantage. Grasping each other's shoulders, they spun around and around, until finally, one of Robard's legs kicked out and caught the other man at the knee. He went down on his back and Robard leapt on top of him.

With his knees on the man's arms, Robard pummeled him with blow after blow, but the bandit was strong and still struggled, whereas Robard was tiring. I rushed forward and put the point of my sword at the man's throat. Even then he fought to free himself.

"Enough!" I said.

Finally his body sagged in defeat. He lay back on the ground, arms and body relaxed but appearing as if he could spring on us at any moment.

Robard pulled at the hood, which fit tightly around the man's face. He yanked and tugged until finally we could see him clearly.

"Oh," said Robard in surprise. "Oh my God! Will? Will Scarlet, is that you?"

18

ho are you?" the man on the ground demanded.

"It's me, Will. Rob. Robard Hode. Surely you recognize me?" he asked.

In confusion I removed my sword from the man's neck. His eyes widened in recognition, and a large and happy smile crossed his face. "Master Robard! Praise God, can it be true?"

"It is, Will. My duty with the King's Archers is over and I'm on my way home. What in the world are you doing? Why did you try to rob us?"

The man stood, dusting himself off, but kept his head down as if ashamed of what had just happened.

"Um, Robard?" I asked cautiously.

"Oh. Yes. Sorry. Tristan, Maryam, everyone, meet Will Scarlet. He is, or at least was when I left, my father's forester."

For a moment Robard's words did not register. "Your father has a forester?" I asked. "I thought you were poor farmers." No farmer I had ever met at St. Alban's or on the nearby plots surrounding it had ever been able to afford a forester, a hired man who managed the workers and lands owned by his thane.

Robard's face colored and he shrugged. "Well, we are poor. I mean in comparison to some of the barons and lords with property surrounding ours." He quickly changed the subject. "Will, why have you taken up thieving? If my father knew of this—"

"Yes, Rob, I know. But, there're things . . . you don't . . . Much has changed, lad, since you've been gone. They've gotten much worse. The crown has raised taxes tenfold and the harvest has been poor these last two years, and since your father . . . Rob, the young lady there, she isn't going to kill poor Allan, is she?" He pointed at Maryam, who still sat astride a bandit, her golden dagger held tightly against his throat.

"What? Oh, no. Maryam, please release him," Robard said.

"I don't like bandits," Maryam said, not moving a muscle.

"These men are not bandits. Not really. So if you would, please don't kill him. His name is Allan Aidale. He also works for my father," Robard said.

"'Lo, everyone," Allan said meekly from the ground.

Maryam let out a disgusted sigh, then stared at Allan, her dark eyes aflame with anger. "Never, ever point a weapon at me again. Understood?" she said to the man pinned beneath her. He nodded vigorously and she stood, sheathing her daggers in one motion. The man scrambled to his feet as Tuck and Little John released their grip on the bandit they had been holding. The man on the ground was still unconscious, and the one I'd chased off had yet to reappear.

"I've known you all my life, Will. Why do you resort to this?" Robard was either very sad or very angry. It was hard to tell.

"Rob . . . I . . . we are hungry and the children of Sherwood are starving. There is a new Shire Reeve in Nottingham. He's worse than the one we had before you left, and he was right bad enough. He's forbiddin' us to hunt without payment to the crown. More than three dozen men from the shire sent off to London town, and we hear tell most have been thrown in the Tower and some even worse. We didn't know if you were alive or dead . . . if you were ever coming back. . . ." Will Scarlet's voice trailed off and I felt sorry for him.

"But Will, surely my father would not stand for this. Where is he? Why is he not setting things straight with this Shire Reeve?" Robard demanded.

Will's shoulders drooped and he stared at the ground. "He's . . . oh, Rob. I don't know how to tell you this. He's gone, Rob."

"Gone? What do you mean? Gone where?" Robard insisted.

"To heaven, Rob. He died the first winter after you left. The Shire Reeve took him to his jail in Nottingham and he died there," Will said softly.

Robard staggered, as if he'd been struck by an invisible hand.

"What? No! You're lying. You thieving bastard!" He took hold of Will's tunic with both hands, pulling him until his face was inches from the frightened man. "You take it back, right now!"

"Master Rob," said Allan, touching him gently on the arm. "I'm afraid so, lad. It happened just as old Will said. Please let him go now. It's not his fault—he did everythin' he could to keep things up, 'opin' you might return one day. But it's been nigh on impossible. Sorry we are about the thievin', but no harm done. Your friend with the sword here put a dreadful fright in poor Gerald, though. I suspect we'll not see him until it's right spring." He tried to laugh to ease the tension, but it just came out as an awkward squawk. Both men looked sad and worn. I guessed they were in their fifties, which made them older than even Tuck or Little John.

Robard's forester, Will Scarlet, had hardly moved, and as he stood in the gathering light of morning, his hair was flecked with gray. He was thin but, like Robard, thick through the arms and chest from many hours pulling a longbow. His hands were scarred and his skin showed age and wrinkles. But when I studied him and Allan, I saw steel in their veins. These unlikely bandits were also hardened men. Despite their flowing cloaks, they had the look of lean and hungry wolves. They were forest men, hunters, fighters, trackers. And they clearly had a deep affection for Robard.

I tried to help. "Robard, please let him go. We can ride on to Sherwood, to your farm. We can puzzle this out. But you need to release him."

Slowly and with barely contained grief, Robard unhanded Will, dropping his fists to his sides. Tears flowed freely down his cheeks.

"Will, tell me the truth, what happened to my father," he finally said.

"It's like I said, Rob. The crown, Prince John mainly, has raised taxes too many times to count in the last two years. Folks, even some of the barons, have lost their lands, their fortunes—there's no money to be had. Men are thrown into prison or sent off to the Crusades like you were, to pay off back taxes. Your father and some of the other landowners finally said 'no more,' and the Shire Reeve and his bailiffs hauled the lot of 'em off to prison. He was there, in Nottingham jail serving his sentence, when he caught a fever and died."

"What happened to our land?" Robard demanded. "Our people, what happened to them?"

"We were barely able to 'old on to the land. The Shire Reeve has taken most of the property around us. With the poor harvests, we've had very little for trade and no one can afford to buy crops anyway. This Shire Reeve is a cruel one. He's taken everyone's land for back taxes and is buying it up himself. He's had his sights on your hides, your land, for a while now, but we've scraped together enough to pay the taxes. There's not much else left over, though, and not enough to feed everyone, so me and the boys, we took matters into our own hands," Will said.

Robard did not hear him, and appeared lost in thought.

"And Rob, please understand. We don't take anythin' from the poor folks of Sherwood. We've robbed those who might have food or crosslets to spare. We take from 'em only what we need to live. The rest goes to the poor families here in the forest. We've been at it a few months. What we've been givin' the poor folk of the shire has made 'em love us. They even call us 'the Merry Men.' Isn't that something?"

"What about my mother? Is she . . . ?"

"She's fine, Master Hode," Allan said. "You know how much the Sherwood people love her. I doubt we'd have kept things up as well as we have if not for her."

Robard's face showed a brief moment of relief, but the anger was back in a heartbeat. He turned on his heel and stalked to his horse, and from his look, I knew what he intended: to ride to Nottingham, find the Shire Reeve and kill him.

My own grief dissipated when I saw my friend's sadness. I stepped in front of him to block his path. "Robard, wait," I pleaded. "I know how you feel—"

"I'm certain you do, squire," he interrupted. "Now get out of my way."

Maryam came to stand beside him and put her hand on his arm. "Robard, you cannot act rashly—"

"If both of you don't leave me be, I swear I will—" he said.

"What about your mother, Robard!" Maryam urged him. That did the trick. His wild eyes came into focus and he stared at her intensely as she reached up and cradled his face in both hands.

"What about my mother?" he asked quietly.

"She has lost a husband. For all she knows you are lost to her as well. You've been gone two years. She has grieved all this time with no son to lean on. She must be desperate and heartbroken. There will be time for vengeance later, Robard. But you must go to her." Maryam's voice was calm, and whatever sea of emotions he felt, she had managed to still them, at least for now.

"My mother," he said. He pushed past me and mounted his horse and urged it to gallop. In a few strides he was invisible, enveloped in the fog. Only the noise of his hoofbeats remained.

"Robard, wait!" I shouted after him. But he was gone.

"Will," I said quietly. He looked confused and sad. "We need to follow Robard. We'll be lost in no time. Can you lead us?"

"Aye. We'll keep after him right enough. Allan, you and the boys fetch our horses. Step quick now. If I know Master Hode, once he pays his respects to Mistress Hode, he'll be a-ridin' to Nottingham and havin' it out with the Shire Reeve himself. Let's go, lads, to your duties," he commanded his men, and they leapt to their work.

Will prodded the poor man on the ground—he called him Cyrus—and he came to with a start, then drew back in fear at the sight of Little John towering over him. "Worry not, Cy, he's a friend. 'Twas Master Hode we tried to rob, can you believe it?" Cyrus allowed as how he could not, and stood, trying to clear his head. Allan and the other man returned with their horses.

"We've given old Rob a good head start, but we'll catch up to 'em soon enough," Allan offered as we all mounted up and rode off with Will Scarlet in the lead. Chasing Robard all the way to his home.

ill and his men were better mounted, and we punished ourselves and our horses trying to keep up with them. But after midday we rode through a gate with a high wooden arch. On it hung a weather-beaten sign with carved letters reading HODE. Passing through it, we followed a long lane lined by very tall trees. Through the trees I saw more woods, but in the distance there were some gently rolling meadows and open fields. It was a beautiful place, and I realized why Robard had been so eager to return home.

We found Robard and his mother not far from their manor house, in a small fenced cemetery standing before a wooden cross. It must have been the family plot where his father was buried. Robard towered over his tiny mother, whose shoulders shook as she cried, and he tried gently to wipe away the river of tears coursing down her face. Our party dismounted in the yard and we all stood quietly, not wishing to disturb them.

Tuck watched the two of them standing by the wooden cross and I wondered if it brought back painful memories of the brothers he had buried not so long ago. Tuck folded his hands in prayer and made his quiet clicking sound before crossing himself. Will and his men, perhaps thinking Tuck was an actual priest from his dress and manor, followed suit.

While Robard tended to his mother, I took stock of the Hode estate. It had fallen on hard times for certain, but it was much grander than a "simple farm," as Robard had led us to believe. The manor house was two stories high, with a large wooden porch running along its front. The steps leading up to it were cracked and loose in a few places, but the thatched roof was in grave disrepair. What had once been glass windows on the front of the house were now boarded up.

Beyond the house lay a barn, a smokehouse and a few smaller outbuildings. The corral next to the barn was missing several lengths of fencing and would have a hard time holding even a small goat. If Hode land was in such a state, I could only imagine what the poorer farmers were experiencing.

Robard and his mother left the small plot and he took her arm, leading her to the yard. His face was drawn and pinched in anger. I felt his grief at what had befallen his mother and his land. We had come here for rest, but there was little peace to be found.

During our travels, Robard had spoken very little of his mother. Despite her circumstances and what must have been her apparent shock at his unexpected return, she showed us a delightful smile. The loss of her husband was tempered by the return of her only child. She could barely take her eyes off of him and followed him around the yard like a puppy. Angel took great delight in meeting Mistress Hode, who fussed over the little mutt as if she were one of her own children.

"Oh, Rob, where ever did you find such a sweet little girl?" his mother cooed, rubbing Angel on the belly.

"A long story," he said. "Mother, there's folk here I need you to welcome. These two in particular have been with me since the Holy Land. Tristan is this scoundrel's name, calls himself a squire to a Templar Knight, but I think it might be a tall tale he's told," Robard said with a twinkle in his eye. He might be angry and upset, but he was not about to forget his manners in front of his mother. He was trying to cheer her up and focus on something besides all the grief.

"You're a friend to my Robin boy?" she asked.

"I am indeed, ma'am," I said.

"Then you are always welcome here," she replied, touching me on the cheek with a tiny wrinkled hand.

"Thank you, ma'am. You are most kind," I said.

Robard introduced his mother to Little John and Brother Tuck, and she was overjoyed to see Tuck in his friar's robes. "It's been far too long a time since we've had a man of God among us here in Sherwood," she said. And when I explained that Tuck could neither speak nor hear, she reached out and patted him gently on the arm, as if it mattered not to her. She considered him a man of the church, and his presence was enough.

Before Robard had even had a chance to introduce her, she took Maryam by the hands.

"Poor lass. Why was it you were forced to travel so far with so many ruffians?"

Maryam, for once, was at a loss for words. She tried to stammer out a reply, but Robard interrupted.

"Mother, this is Maryam. We've been through some scrapes,

the three of us, trying to get home. She can fight and I've seen her best more warriors than I can count. She's saved my skin a dozen times. There's a lot I need to tell you when there's time."

"It's fine, Rob," his mother said. "I could tell when you looked at her the first time that you're quite taken with the lass and her with you. A mother knows these things."

"What?" Robard burst out. "Oh no, it's not like that. Maryam is . . . She's a . . . I'm not taken. No ma' . . ."

"Really?" said Mistress Hode.

"Really . . . ," said Maryam, her eyes as sharp as her daggers. Robard stared at me helplessly. I only shrugged.

Mistress Hode took Maryam by the hand again. "Lass, are you a Christian?"

Maryam swallowed, then quietly answered, "No, ma'am, I'm not."

"But my Rob says you've stood by him, fought at his side. This is true?" she asked.

"Yes, Mistress Hode, it's true. He's a little rough around the edges sometimes, and he's not quite as good with a longbow as he believes, but I've never met a braver or more loyal soul," Maryam said.

Mistress Hode beamed and pulled Maryam toward the house. "'Tis good enough for me. Come, lass, I mean no offense, but you've been riding hard for a long while and I'll bet it's been some time since you've had a proper bath. My maid will draw us water and we'll have a nice chat. Allan, Will, there's a bit of venison left up in the smokehouse. If you two wouldn't mind, you might hunt us a roebuck for our evening meal, although Lord knows there's not many deer left, with everyone as hungry as they are. We don't have much," she said to Maryam and Little John, "but we'll feast this evening. Will, you and the rest to your jobs now. My Robin boy is home, and for one night at least, Sherwood will know no sorrow. Off with you!"

Pulling Maryam behind her, Mistress Hode disappeared into the house with Angel at her heels. Will, Allan and the other men attended to everything needing to be done. They led the horses toward the pasture behind the barn. A large cook fire was lighted in the pit, and before long it was just Robard, Tuck, Little John and me standing in the yard.

"What now?" I asked.

"Now we give my mother her celebration. There's been enough crying today. Tomorrow, I'll ride to Nottingham and speak to this Shire Reeve."

"Robard . . ."

"No, Tristan. Enough talk. Look at the state of my home. If my father were alive, he'd die of disgrace. What of my poor mother having to live like this with the house and everything else falling down around her? Will and Allan have to scrape up whatever they can just to feed the hungry. We'll have words, this Shire Reeve and I. Of that I assure you."

With that, Robard stalked off and disappeared behind the house.

"I think young Hode is asking for trouble," Little John remarked.

"Yes, he needs to take leave and think. We're in no shape to make another enemy of the Shire Reeve," I said.

"You'll stand with him against the Reeve?" Little John asked.

The breeze picked up just then and a small dusting of snow whipped up into the air and blew across the ground at us. I felt the wind cut through me, and if I had not been raised by Christian men, I would have thought it a sign, an omen of evil things to come. Despite my upbringing, for a moment I *did* think so. Something bad was coming our way.

Little John, if he saw any of it, said nothing. I looked him in the eye. "All the way," I said. "All the way."

20

he celebration lasted late into the night. Given the circumstances, and not wanting to upset him, I avoided talking with Robard about his desire to seek out the man responsible for his father's death. Will Scarlet came back with a deer he had shot in the forest. It was cleaned and cooked, and we enjoyed a spartan but delicious meal at Mistress Hode's table. It was easy to see how much Robard enjoyed being home, and I cursed fate for taking his father from him and spoiling his return.

I caught Maryam studying him carefully, knowing as did I how hot tempered and capable of rash acts he was. Yet as the night wore on, he appeared to relax somewhat, as if the edge of his anger had dulled, and when the time for sleep arrived, I thought perhaps he would have a clearer head come morning.

Maryam had bathed and washed and combed her hair, and she wore a new tunic Mistress Hode had somehow found and altered to fit her. Her cloak had been washed and mended, and Maryam looked positively radiant. She laughed and joked with Robard and the men, and they obviously enjoyed her company, though it was evident she also made them nervous, as they remembered her skill with daggers.

When our meal ended, Tuck, Little John and I made beds on the floor of the main room of the manor house, near the fireplace. We offered to sleep in the barn, but Mistress Hode would have none of it. Robard went to his room in the back of the house, and Will, Allan and the others departed for their own homes on the property. Maryam was given a bed in the upper level next to Mistress Hode's sleeping quarters. We fell fast asleep. It had been an eventful day and we were all exhausted. Sleeping indoors, even on the hard floor, covered by the warm quilts provided us, was a welcome treat.

I'm not sure what awakened me in the early morning hours. My sleep was usually deep and undisturbed, but perhaps a creak of a floorboard or the whispered sound of clothing passing nearby brought me to my senses. The fire was a bed of coals and the orange light gave off a soft glow, lighting the room just enough to see dim shapes. I heard the snores of Tuck and John, then the front door creak slowly open and shut. I stood and investigated immediately. I had slept in my clothes, and only needed to buckle on my sword as I crept quietly through the house.

When I stepped through the door, I scanned the yard to see who was about this hour and caught a glimpse of Robard heading into the barn where the horses were stabled. My suspicions were confirmed. He had not given up on his intention of confronting the Shire Reeve but hoped to sneak away. Doing so would prevent his mother, Maryam and me from trying to talk him out of it.

The night air was cold and the ground was covered in thick

frost. The half moon was low in the sky, so daybreak was still some hours away. A few flakes of snow flew about on the breeze, but the sky was clearing and cloudless toward the east.

Following Robard to the barn, I made no attempt to keep silent. The three of us had been traveling for months, always on guard, ever alert for danger, and surprising a King's Archer in the dead of night was never a good idea. He had closed the barn door behind him and I opened it and stepped inside. A small oil lamp burned from a hanger on a post near the horse stalls, but Robard was nowhere to be seen.

"Robard?" I called out. He did not answer.

"Robard, it's me, Tristan. I know where you're going. Don't do it alone. Let's talk about it first." The barn remained silent.

I stepped farther in and looked up at the loft where hay was stacked. I strained to see into the darkened corners but still did not find my friend. How had he disappeared?

"Robard, I know you can hear me. Believe me when I say I understand your feelings. We've both lost—" For a moment the words would not come as an image of the crosses lining the lane at St. Alban's flooded my memory and grief briefly threatened to take over again.

"Just know I share your sorrow, but please, I beg of you, do not do this."

There was another small door leading to the corral outside directly across from me, and I wondered for an instant if perhaps I had misjudged Robard's intent. Maybe he had been unable to sleep and had merely gone for a walk to clear his head. But I discounted the thought; he would not have left a lamp burning where a fire could easily start.

Just as I was about to call out to him again, I felt a hand on my shoulder. I jumped in fright. "Don't do that—" I said, turning to face Robard. But before I could ask him where he thought he was going, his gloved fist shot out and connected solidly with my jaw, and I fell to the ground unconscious.

Something poked me in the chest and my eyes opened wide. "Robard, stop it. This is no time—" I looked up and found not Robard, but his mother, Little John, Maryam, Angel and Will all staring down at me. There was enough light to see them clearly, which meant it must be early morning. I sat up. Little John reached out to pull me to my feet.

"Where is my son?" his mother asked me as I rubbed my aching jaw.

"He's gone?" I asked Will.

"Aye, he's nowhere about, Master Tristan. We've looked everywhere," Will answered.

"Where's the tree?" Little John asked, smirking slightly at my bruised face.

"I beg your pardon?" I replied.

"The one you walked into. Looks like you took a nasty shot. Was it courtesy of your friend?"

"Yes," I said with a sigh. "I heard him leaving the house early this morning. I worried he was on his way to Nottingham. Tried to stop him, but he sneaked up on me and knocked me out. I don't know how long he's been gone."

"What a fool. When I get my hands on him . . ." Maryam stopped, her cheeks coloring, remembering Robard's mother.

"No worries, lass. He takes after his father, he does. Stubborn as a stump he was, and Rob is a bit of the bark off the same tree . . ." Mistress Hode shook her head and clasped her hands together in worry. "He can't stand against the Shire Reeve, foolish boy. He has fifty bailiffs if he has one. What am I going to do?" Tears formed in her eyes, and my heart melted in my chest. In just the short time I'd known her, I'd seen her love and kindness go out to everyone she knew and met. Her son's homecoming had brought her great joy after what must have been horrible months of loneliness and sorrow. Robard was my friend in fact and brother in spirit, if not in blood. Right then I decided I would bring him back to her. Alive.

"Don't you worry, Mistress Hode. We'll go fetch him."

I reached out to put my hand on her shoulder and she instead took me in a fierce embrace, her small head buried in my chest. The thick wool of my cloak muffled her sobs. "Dear God in heaven, thank you, boy. Please do. Bring him back to me."

"Will, we'll need you to lead us there, if you agree." I looked at him. From what I'd seen of him in our short time together, he'd be someone I'd want on my side in a fight. This was his territory, and Allan and the others would look to him before they ever followed me.

"Aye, lad. I know the way. And if you're willing to lead, I'm with you. Allan and the rest of the thane's men will follow too, once I tell 'em 'tis so. We'll fight for Robard and Mistress Hode and any other of our folk. Me and the boys, we did all right floatin' through Sherwood and pinchin' a purse or two. But you're a soldier, and if we face the Shire Reeve, then I beg you to do the thinkin'."

"All right then," I said. "Thank you, Will. If you'll see to your men? The rest of us will make ready." Will left the barn on the run.

"Little John, I know you and Robard had your differences and this certainly isn't your fight. But if you're willing, we sure could use your help."

Little John stroked his thick beard, his staff held in one giant hand. For a moment, I thought he would beg off and take to the road again, which would certainly be his right. But then he smiled. "Why not? I'm already a wanted man. What's a few more laws broken?" With a twinkle in his eye, he patted Robard's mother gently on the head. "Besides, don't tell him, but I've taken a liking to young Robard. He's got spunk, he does. Might get all riled up now and then, but he's a fighter. I'm in."

"Excellent. Let's get the horses saddled and be on our way. Mistress Hode, would you be kind enough to fetch Brother Tuck? I'll want him along with us."

In a few minutes we had the horses fed and watered and saddled. While we waited for Will's return, Maryam took time to sharpen her daggers on a whetstone in the barn. Robard had left Sir Thomas' battle sword behind and I lent it to John. He drew it from the scabbard and swung it once or twice, and it looked like a toy in his hand. Angel paced back and forth nervously in the yard, as if she knew Robard was missing. Tuck came to the barn with Mistress Hode and we walked our horses out to the yard, waiting for Will and the others. They arrived a few moments later.

"Tristan," Mistress Hode said to me as we all mounted up and prepared to ride. "You be right careful. Robard's father ran afoul of this man the first day he met him. He's vain, vicious and evil, he is. His name is William Wendenal and you will find no viler a creature on God's earth. Watch your step, young squire, we're about to run out of men here in Sherwood. Take care, now, and bring my Robard home."

"We'll be careful," I said, telling her not to worry as we rode away.

After all, I thought as the faces of Sir Hugh, the Queen Mother, Richard the Lionheart and the High Counsel of Languedoc crossed my thoughts, standing against the vain and evil was apparently my specialty.

21

ottingham was a smaller, more compact version of Dover. The difference was accentuated by Nottingham's location here in the dense, wooded north country, whereas Dover lay by the coast, making it appear even larger with the sea as a backdrop. Nottingham still had a good-size marketplace and lots of shops and other buildings clustered together in a center square. But as we had seen in other towns and villages along our journey north, hard times had come here as well, and there wasn't the level of activity and commerce you might expect. It was quiet, with only a few vendors visible in the square and small groups of people milling about.

"What day is it, Will?" I asked.

"I don't rightly know, my lord. We tend to lose track of 'em out here in the woods. We've no priest at Sherwood now, and we can't even keep track of the Holy Days, may the saints forgive us," he said.

"I'm sure they have already, Will. I just wondered if it might be Sunday. And please stop calling me 'lord.' I'm most definitely not a noble." He smiled and shrugged and stared down at the town. We would draw unneeded attention if we rode into town on the Sabbath carrying weapons and bristling for a fight. But there appeared to be enough people about to indicate it was not a Sunday.

"Where will we find the Shire Reeve?" I asked. "And is there anything else you can tell me about him?"

"He keeps at the constabulary. It's here in the tall tower near the center of town and the jail is next to it. He came here straight from Prince John's court, 'tis told," Will said, pointing out the building. "Like the mistress said, he's a vile man, vain and pompous when you meet him. That's all I can tell you, sire. Except if he catches any one of me or the boys, we'll dangle from the rope for certain."

"Let's try not to let that happen then. Something tells me we'll find Robard at the constabulary," I said. "Onward."

We cantered down the rise and into the village. The few people on the streets paid us little mind, and we stopped and dismounted outside a small inn about fifty yards away from the jail. Sure enough, Robard's horse was tied to a hitching post right outside the building.

"How many bailiffs does the Shire Reeve have available to him, Will?" I asked.

"I don't rightly know, lad. 'Tis many more of 'em than us," he said. "I expect with times as hard as they are, a lot of men are signin' on, working for food and board."

Another ideal situation, I thought. We were outnumbered and I was in unfamiliar territory. Straightening my tunic, I reached into my satchel, removing Sir Thomas' ring and slipping it onto my finger. I stomped what mud I could from my boots and pulled my sword forward on my belt, trying to make myself presentable.

"What are you going to do?" Maryam asked.

"I'm not sure yet," I said. "You wait here. Try to draw as little attention as possible. Little John, if you would, position the men across the street from the jail and keep a sharp eye. Will, it's best if you and your men look disinterested. Don't string any bows or nock any arrows yet, but be ready. Robard has probably been thrown in jail already, and I'm going to have to get him out—one way or another. Maryam, you stay with John and watch the door. If I'm not out in a reasonable amount of time, the two of you had best enter the constabulary and . . . help. Come on, Angel," I said. She sat up and, although tired from her long and vigorous trek, eagerly loped along beside me.

Walking down the street, I attempted to appear important and determined, in case anyone was observing my approach. The front door of the constabulary was unguarded, and I entered without knocking. Inside I found a dim room, with meager light coming from two windows on either side of the door. The walls held oil lamps, but the plank wood floor and lack of any furniture or decorations gave the room a dismal, fearful quality.

"Hello!" I shouted out.

A hallway led away from the main room, and the sound of footsteps echoed on the wooden floor. A few seconds later, a tall, thin man entered. He was splendidly dressed, with a purple velvet tunic, immaculate white leggings and a dark red cape draped around his shoulders. His eyes were ice blue, and his beard was neatly trimmed and flecked with gray. It was hard to guess his age, but he had the appearance of confidence. If this was the Shire Reeve, he would not be easily persuaded.

He stared at me in total disdain but did not speak.

"I seek the Shire Reeve of Nottingham," I said.

"You have found him," he said.

"Ah, thank you, sire," I said. "I'm Tristan of St. Alban's of the Poor Fellow Soldiers of Christ and King Solomon's Temple and I—"

"You're a Knight of the Temple?" he sneered, hardly believing me. Angel, sitting at my side, let out a low growl. I shushed her, and he glanced down and blanched, as if I'd committed a mortal sin by bringing a dog into his constabulary.

"Oh no, sire, not a knight, certainly. I'm a squire, actually, but I've been sent here on a matter of utmost urgency to the Order. I'm in pursuit of a man," I said, spinning my web.

"And how does this concern me?" he asked.

"Well, sire, his name is Robard Hode, of Sherwood Forest. He has recently returned home from distinguished service in the Crusades and . . . may I have your name, sire?" I asked.

The man sniffed. "My name is William Wendenal. And your Robard Hode arrived here but a short while ago, making many wild accusations. He was subdued by my bailiffs and now resides in my jail. I hardly believe such a ruffian would be of any interest to the Order."

"I understand, sire, I rightly do. And from what I've heard he is a hot-tempered sort. But there's Order business involving Master Hode I must see to. I've a letter here from my knight, Sir Thomas Leux. It asks anyone whom I encounter for their assistance, with the thanks and praise of the Templar Knights." I removed Sir Thomas' letter from my satchel, hoping the oil-skin had preserved it well enough that it was still readable. Why hadn't I checked it before I came in? But there was no time now. I handed it to Wendenal with Sir Thomas' ring showing on my finger. I sincerely hoped it would be enough to convince him I was a legitimate *servante* of the Order.

It was not.

"Do you take me for a fool, boy?" he sneered, shoving the parchment back at me without even reading it.

"I assure you, sire, I do not," I replied with as much earnestness as I could muster.

"Good. Then you will understand perfectly well when I tell you I have no intention of releasing my prisoner to you." He thrust Sir Thomas' letter into my hand.

"That is most unfortunate, sire. What can I do to convince you of the seriousness of this matter?" I pleaded.

"Nothing. Now, take your dog and leave or I shall have my bailiffs escort you out."

With a heavy sigh, I rolled up Sir Thomas' parchment letter and returned it to the satchel.

"I'm sorry to have disturbed you, sire," I said. "However, if I may have one more moment of your time." The Shire Reeve already had turned his back to me. When he looked over his shoulder, his eyes flew open wide at the sight of my sword mere inches from his neck.

"What is the meaning of this!" he demanded.

"I'm afraid I must insist you take me to the prisoner at once."

on't make a sound," I said. "Do not alert your bailiffs or so help me you will lose an ear." I kept my voice low. Angel stood and growled, moving quickly to the hallway and sniffing the air.

"Quiet, girl," I said to her.

"You are a fool," the Shire Reeve whispered. "My bailiffs—"

I pushed the sword closer to his neck and his words died in his throat.

"One sound from you, a shout, even a heavy sigh and I will run you through," I said. "Do you understand me, sire? This can be over quickly, with no harm done if you pay attention. How many bailiffs are on duty in the jail?"

"I won't tell you any—" he stammered, but another jab from my sword persuaded him to speak the truth. "There are two. Only two."

"Excellent," I said. "Now, you will turn and walk silently down the hallway. You will take us directly to Master Hode and you will not call out or warn anyone, is that clear?"

"You won't—"

"Is that clear!?" I said through clenched teeth, moving the sword ever closer to his throat.

With exaggerated care, William Wendenal, the Shire Reeve of Nottingham, turned and walked down the hallway. Angel took the lead, her nose constantly working the air, and I followed behind him, my sword point pressed against the small of his back. The hallway was as spartan as the room we had just left. Over the Shire Reeve's shoulder I could see light ahead as it led to a bigger room, which must be the jail.

Angel gave a low whine and I assumed it was because she smelled men ahead, or perhaps she had caught Robard's scent. I shushed her and we kept moving forward.

"I have the authority to hang you for this," Wendenal said.

"Sire, there is a long list of people far more powerful than you who have threatened to hang me, and yet I'm still here. Be silent."

The walk down the hallway took an eternity. With every step I second-guessed myself. My heart was hammering in my chest as we stepped into a large room with stone walls and a series of iron-barred cells along the rear wall. Two bailiffs sat at a large table to my left. At first they didn't understand the situation, but once they observed my sword pointed at the back of the Shire Reeve, they jumped to their feet, drawing their own blades.

"The first of you to move against me will have your reeve's blood on his hands," I said as calmly as I could.

They stood stock-still. When I chanced a glance at the cells, my heart sank, then pounded with rage. There were three of them, each nearly ten feet on a side. And they were full of men, at least ten or fifteen in each cage. They were dirty and ragged, and their smell nearly overwhelmed me. They were so crowded together there was barely room for any of them to move.

"What have these men done to be treated so?" I demanded.

"They have refused or proved unable to pay their properly levied taxes to the crown," the Shire Reeve insisted.

"My God. And you think you've the right to lock them up like animals?" I nearly cried.

"They have broken the law. There is—"

"Enough!" I interrupted him.

I couldn't spot Robard through the crowded cells. They were too full of men. But Angel found him. She barged forward to the center cell and wormed her way through the bars. Startled, the men inside moved aside as she ran to Robard, who was sitting against the rear wall. He was in bad shape. He appeared to have been beaten severely and sat with his head slumped forward on his chest, but when Angel jumped into his lap, he raised his head and gazed at me through swollen eyes.

"I was wondering when you'd get here," he groaned.

"Can you stand? Walk?" I asked.

He nodded and two men in his cell helped him to his feet.

"Sorry about your jaw," he said.

"Don't worry. Maryam hits harder than you." I laughed as I spoke, and so did he. And it might be true: Maryam did hit awfully hard.

Watching him limp slowly toward the door, my blood boiled. If I had not sworn to obey the Templar Code, I would have struck down the Shire Reeve, defenseless or not.

"Instruct your men to unlock the cells," I ordered.

I expected token resistance or another warning of the rope

155

awaiting me, but Wendenal shrugged toward the bailiff with a large set of iron keys on his belt, and he obediently opened the middle cell door.

"Come, Robard, we have places to be," I said.

"A moment, Tristan," he said as he walked through the door of his cell. I thought the bailiff might strike him down, but with another glance in my direction he stayed his hand. Robard snatched away first his sword and then the keys.

As quickly as his weakened state would allow, he unlocked the remaining cell doors.

"All of you are free. Leave now. Return to your homes and families. If you've a mind, join me in Sherwood. Thanks to this man, we don't have much, but we'll share what we have. If you're no friend to tyranny, find me there," he said.

Some of the men, exhausted and abused as they were, remained still, too afraid to move. But eventually they filed out of their cells. Some of them limping and moving gingerly, a few helping the sick and infirm. Slowly at first, then more rapidly they filed past me and down the hallway to the constabulary.

Robard prodded the bailiff into the cell with his own sword. Suddenly, the other bailiff made a move. Angel barked in warning and I shouted. Wendenal tried to squirm away, but I grabbed him by the collar of his cape and held him firmly, making sure he could feel my sword at his back. As the bailiff advanced, Robard threw open the cell door, catching the man square in the face. He tumbled to the ground like a sack of potatoes.

Groaning with the effort, Robard dragged the unconscious man into the center cell and locked him in.

"All right, Shire Reeve," he said. "In you go."

"You are insane. I will see you both hang for this," Wendenal sputtered.

I pushed him forward roughly and he stumbled into the last remaining empty cell. Robard turned the key in the lock and smiled, though it appeared to cause him pain. He shuffled across the room and stuffed the keys in his belt, then snatched up his bow and wallet from where they had been stacked in the corner.

"I will find you," Wendenal said through the bars, his voice full of rage. "My men and I will hunt you down and you will both hang."

Robard walked back to the cell, staring at Wendenal through the bars.

"My name is Robard Hode, son of Robard Hode the second, and I consider you his murderer. I'm returning to my land in Sherwood Forest, and if you intend to hang me, find me there if you can, or dare. Enjoy your stay in your own jail, Shire Reeve." Robard limped over to me, putting his hand on my shoulder. His face was bruised and scratched, and it was difficult for him to move, though he tried not to show it.

"I knew you'd come for me," he said.

"You'd do the same. In fact, you already have."

"Aye. So what do you suggest we do next?" he asked.

"Run," I said.

"That's the best plan I think you've ever had," he said.

So, with Angel barking and leading us down the hallway, and as quickly as Robard's wounds would allow, we ran.

We had not reached the front room before the shouts of Wendenal and his bailiffs rang out. We burst through the door into the street and squinted at the light. Maryam raced to Robard's side and

157

pulled him into a fierce embrace. There was joy on her face mixed with the rage she felt at seeing him so beaten. For a moment, I toyed with the idea of sending Maryam into the jail with her daggers and letting her settle with the Shire Reeve.

Tuck and John joined our little group, and across the street I saw Will and his men stand ready, drawing arrows. Tuck quickly examined Robard's arms and hands and shook his head to me while making a motion with his hands as if he were snapping a twig in two.

"Tuck says you have nothing broken," I said.

"Really? Have him check again if you don't mind, for I certainly feel as if I do." Robard smiled grimly. This only caused Maryam to hug him harder and this time he squawked in pain. "Easy, Maryam. You win this round," he joked.

Allan approached quickly with our horses.

"Little John, I expect a few men will be shortly coming out the door there. Would you stand ready?" I asked.

As we helped Robard into the saddle, a window above the jail crashed open and a crossbow poked through. "Ho!" Will shouted in alarm. He and three of his men stepped forward from their hiding places and sent a hail of arrows at the window, driving the man there back in retreat before he could get a shot off.

The door to the jail crashed open and two bailiffs rushed out. "Halt in the na—" one of them tried to say, but Little John's staff took the man square in the gut and drove him to the ground. The man behind him had his sword at the ready, but before he could move, Little John snapped the end of his staff into his jaw and he fell to the muddy street unconscious. The downed man tried to stand, but John drove a very large fist into his jaw, and he collapsed and moved no more. Very quickly Little John produced a small length of rope from his tunic and wrapped one end securely through the large wooden handle on the door. He tied the other end tightly to a nearby hitching post, which effectively made the door impossible to open from the inside.

Curious onlookers gathered in the street outside the jail, and when they saw Little John and Will Scarlet besting the Shire Reeve's men, many of them cheered. The noise brought more villagers to investigate the commotion. Before he mounted his horse, Allan Aidale climbed up on top of a nearby barrel and shouted, "Why, it must be the Merry Men we've heard tell of! They've come to test the Shire Reeve! Only they could stand against him!" And he exhorted the crowd to chant, "Merry Men! Merry Men!"

With the cheers of the townsfolk ringing in our ears we goaded our horses to run and rode hard and fast for Sherwood Forest.

23

obard," I asked as we galloped along, "do you think this is a good idea?"

"What?" he said through gritted teeth. I felt his misery. My side still ached from my wound, though Tuck's salves had made it considerably better. I knew how painful it was to ride a horse in such a condition.

"Riding straight to Sherwood? Why don't we hide out somewhere else?"

"We could, but where would we go?" he countered. "In Sherwood, we have places to hide, the people are on our side, and we know the terrain far better than he does. It will give us a great advantage. Besides, we can't leave my mother unprotected."

I supposed Robard was right, but I couldn't help but worry. We had managed to make another powerful enemy, and I was sure, once the Shire Reeve put out news of us, that Sir Hugh would hear of our exploits here. He wouldn't care a whit about Sherwood's people or terrain or anything else. He would strike at us no matter where we decided to hide.

We rode on in silence. There was nothing to say. We needed

to put space between ourselves and Nottingham. Then we needed rest and food. And a plan.

The woods deepened as we rode on through the remaining daylight. Though it was winter, the trees grew thicker and the stark beauty of the landscape revealed itself. This forest must be glorious in spring and summer, I thought as we rode along.

Toward twilight, we steered off the main trail and cut into the woods before pulling up at a spring to water the horses. Robard nearly tumbled from the saddle, then walked stiff legged back and forth, trying to work the soreness out of his bones. While we waited, Will and his men made a thorough check of the horses, inspecting their hooves and forelegs.

"They're nearly ready to give out, Rob," Will said to Robard.

"I know. Not much farther, though," Robard replied.

I watched in fascination as Allan shinnied up a nearby tree. He kept climbing high into the branches.

"What is he doing?" I asked.

"Watch," Robard said.

He finally reached a spot where the tree branches split off into two massive limbs, reached inside a hollow in the trunk of the tree and removed a small bundle wrapped in some kind of cloth, and then another, dropping them where they were carefully caught by one of Will's men. As Allan scampered down, the other men unwrapped each of the bundles to reveal perhaps three dozen arrows.

I shook my head in amazement as Robard and Will and the rest replenished their wallets with a fresh supply of shafts. I marveled at their ingenuity.

Shortly after nightfall, we rode back into the yard of the Hodes' manor house. Mistress Hode was overcome with relief as she ran down the steps and pulled Robard into a hug so strong that Robard cried out in pain.

"Oh! Easy, Mother, I'm a little bruised up," he said, trying to smile.

As quickly as she embraced him, she stepped free and then whacked him hard across the cheek.

"Ow! What was that for?" he cried.

She smacked him again, but he saw that one coming and put up his arms to block her.

"You stubborn, pigheaded, foolish man! Just like your father, only you are worse! What were you thinking to give me such a fright? Riding off to get yourself killed when you've just come back to me? I should cut me a length of birch and give your thick hide the tanning it deserves!"

Robard looked sheepish.

"You are thane now, Robard. Your folk look to you for guidance and protection the very same way they did your father and his before him. And what is it you do first chance you get? Traipse off to pick a fight. You're lucky he didn't hang you!" She had worked up a real temper, and Robard soon realized there was nothing to do but let her run it out.

"I'm sorry, Mother," Robard said quietly. This brought another rain of blows, which he tried to duck beneath as much as his sore body would allow.

"I'll show you sorry! I've met horses what have more sense than you! I can't do it, Robin boy. I lost your father, and I'll not lose you," she cried, and with tears on her cheeks, she ran back to the house.

We stood there in shocked silence, and then Maryam faced Robard.

"I haven't seen her so angry since—" but he never got to finish his thought, for Maryam's right fist came out of nowhere and connected with the point of his chin. Completely unprepared, Robard flew backward, landing on the cold ground.

"I agree with everything your mother said. And if you ever do anything like this again, you'll wish you were back in that cell." She left him sprawled on the ground and followed Mrs. Hode into the house.

Little John was suddenly consumed with a coughing fit, which sounded an awful lot like muffled laughter behind his giant fist. Robard gazed up at me in wonderment, hoping for some kind of explanation.

"Don't look at me," I said as I helped him to his feet. "Grew up in a monastery, remember?"

Robard shrugged and tried to stretch his aching back. He had a serious look on his face, but was clearly happy to be home.

"Mr. John Little," Robard said, putting out his hand, "I owe you an apology. You stood by us, and came to my aid in Nottingham when I did nothing to deserve it. Tristan, as usual, was right about you."

Little John took Robard's hand with no hesitation. "No harm, lad. What happened on that old bridge is behind us as far as I'm concerned. But now you're safe home, and I'd best be moving on."

"About that," Robard interrupted. "You're welcome to stay if you like. As you can see, there's work needs to be done here. A man with a steady hand could find plenty to do. Tristan and Maryam and I will be leaving for a short while, and I'd like someone to keep an eye on things. Will's a good man, but he belongs in the fields and forest. There's no pay, but you'll have food and a roof over your head, if you're willing. Whenever there's real money to be had, I give you my word you'll be treated fairly."

Little John didn't need to take long to consider Robard's offer. "Best offer I've had in a while." They shook hands. "If you don't mind, I'd like to begin. I think I'll have a look at your forge in the barn. Tristan, I expect after what happened in town, you and Robard here have a lot to talk about. So maybe you can tell Tuck to come with me, and we'll take stock and see what needs to be done before the Shire Reeve shows up."

There wasn't much daylight left, but I took Tuck's hand and pointed to Little John and the distant barn, and he immediately understood. He took Charlemagne by the reins and followed obediently.

"He's right," I said, glancing after them. "We have to get ready, Robard. The Shire Reeve will be coming after us. He won't allow what we did to go unpunished. And I'm sure he'll send word to the court of Prince John asking for funds to raise more bailiffs. He'll offer a reward for the both of us. And if news of our exploits reaches the court, you know it will be whispered into Sir Hugh's ear."

I felt guilty. Remembering what Sir Hugh had done to St. Alban's, even before he knew I had the Grail, made me shudder. The thought of his bringing vengeance down on Robard and his family was more than I could bear.

"It might be best if I left," I said. "If I head out on my own and make myself visible, make a trail for Sir Hugh to follow, he might not come here. It would still leave you to handle the Shire Reeve.

Maybe it might be better for everyone if you took your mother and found a place to hide in the forest."

Robard stared at me, disgusted.

"Are you mad? First, I will never give up Hode land without a fight. Second, you wouldn't last a day trying to make your way out of here to the north through Scotland alone. Now listen to me, for this is the last time I'm going to say it. I made a promise to you, swearing to be with you to the end. Nothing has changed. Not some Shire Reeve or Sir Hugh or anything else will come between us and finishing our job. Are we clear?"

My eyes nearly watered, but I nodded.

"Good. It's settled. Come with me, there's something I want to show you," he said. "But first, I also want to apologize for what happened in the barn this morning. It's just . . . I knew you'd talk me out of it, and I was so blind with anger, I couldn't let you. It was all I could think to do. I hope you'll forgive me," he said, holding out his hand. I shook it, assuring him I did.

We strolled up the steps of the porch and entered the house. Inside the door was a series of pegs made from deer antlers where Robard hung up his bow and wallet. I removed my swords and followed him into the main room where I'd slept the night before. At the far end stood a fireplace, and above it a large sword rested on two wooden pegs.

Robard pulled the sword down and handed it to me. It was old—I could tell by the worn leather of the hilt and the marks and nicks upon the steel. But the edge was still sharp, and I felt the heft of it in my hand. It was not as large as Sir Thomas' battle sword, but it had once been a fine weapon.

"This sword belonged to my grandfather's grandfather,"

Robard said. "He carried it at Hastings when Harold took on Willy Bastard. It was luck and treachery that brought victory to the Norman swine that day."

"It's beautiful," I said. Robard took it back from me.

"Yes it is, and it has hung here since he returned more than one hundred years ago. We Hodes have always answered the call of King and Country even when the king is a wretch, like the Lionheart." Robard spat in the fireplace at the mention of Richard. "My family has lived on this very spot for hundreds of years. My ancestors pushed back Viking raiders and we fought willingly with the Saxon kings. But William changed everything. Still he won the fight and called himself King, and we Hodes swore our allegiance and continued to support the crown. My father used to say there wasn't a Norman king worth half a crosslet until King Henry II. Yet we did our duty. Father said, 'You fight for the throne, not always the man who sits on it.' And when we couldn't pay the taxes the crown asked of us, we made an agreement and honored it. I served and gave the Lionheart two years of my life for forgiveness of my father's debt."

"I'm not sure I understand your point, Robard," I said.

"My point is this: I rode into Nottingham aflame, ready to strike down William Wendenal for what he'd done to my father. Like I usually do, I went straight at him full of anger and not thinking. His bailiffs clubbed me down and threw me in his jail with the rest of my countrymen and he took joy in quoting the law to me. It was taxes this and levies that and those of us in those cells were nothing but ignorant peasants who weren't entitled to anything but what the crown grants us, if that." He held the sword up so I could see it clearly.

"William Wendenal will come for me in force, and I'll beat him back, make him wish he'd never heard the name Hode. But my defeating him won't solve a thing. While I sat there in the jail cell, I realized the law is on his side. No matter what I say or do, it's what's written down that matters. And I can't fight it, because I don't even know what I'm fighting. You have to understand your enemy before you can defeat him, and my enemy is not the Shire Reeve of Nottingham, it's the laws he represents."

"I understand, Robard, but what can you do?" I asked.

"I need to know what it is I'm fighting, Tristan. For the many years we Hodes have lived here, we've done right by the land and our people. We took a fair piece of each man's harvest who worked our hides, our plots of land. In return they received our protection. In hard times and bad harvests everyone took less to get by. Justice was decided based on what was fair and true, and every man had a chance to speak his piece before his peers, no matter what he might be accused of. Before I left for war, there were more than thirty families working Hode land, and my father and his father before him never made a decision without thinking what was right for our folk. It was our way, but it's gone. Now we sit at the mercy of some king and his Shire Reeves who do nothing but throw words at us. Words we cannot understand." He knelt and poked at the logs in the fire, stirring the coals so the flames caught again.

"Robard, what is it you seek? How can I help?" I asked.

When he stood, his expression was as serious as I've ever seen it.

"My father is gone, Tristan. I'm the thane now, and I'll lose our lands for sure if I can't learn these laws and throw their own words back at them. I'll fight for my land and my people, and I'll die for them if I must and not think twice, but if there's one thing the Lionheart taught me, it is that if you're going to fight, fight smart."

He put his hands on his hips and stared at the flames a few minutes.

"I don't ask this lightly, Tristan, and I'll thank you not to laugh at my request," he said.

"Of course not, Robard," I said.

It took him a moment as several emotions crawled across his face. Pride, anger, frustration and embarrassment, but finally determination.

"Tristan, I want you to teach me to read."

he night had warmed somewhat from the colder weather earlier in the day. We sat around the large cook fire and enjoyed Mistress Hode's supper. It was meager food, with very little meat, but she did make a hearty venison stew and had baked fresh bread in anticipation of our return. Once she was over her anger about Robard's rash adventure, her spirits returned. While she sat by the fire eating, with Maryam at her side, Mistress Hode regaled us all with funny stories of Robard as a child.

"When he was just a wee lad, couldn't have been more than four, his father made him a small bow and cut the points off some arrows for him to practice with. He loved it. He marched around the fields shooting at any target he could find. One morning he decided to go out to the pasture behind the barn to hunt. Master Hode had raised a bull from a calf, he called him Henry after the king, and as far as Henry was concerned, none of us Hodes were welcome in his field. What made it worse was Robard decidin' he wanted to hunt old Henry. He didn't know them arrows weren't going to stick in that tough hide and all they would do is make him angry." She started to chuckle and Robard's face reddened.

"Mother, please—" he pleaded. But everyone shushed him.

"The next thing you hear is Robin boy hollerin' as loud as he could. 'Twas near on dinnertime his father and I stood right here in this very spot and look up to see him running as fast as his tiny legs would carry him. It had rained the night before and Robard runs straight for the corral fence with Ol' Henry not more'n a few steps behind. He dives headfirst through the fence and lands facedown in the mud. Covered him from head to toe, it did!" She laughed and we laughed with her, and even Robard joined in.

Before the meal, Little John, Maryam and Robard and I had discussed what to do about the Shire Reeve. We all agreed he would be coming soon, and we needed to make ready.

"When do you think he'll make his move?" Little John asked.

"As soon as he can gather his bailiffs and equip them. I would feel better if I knew how many men he had available," I said.

After more discussion, Robard set Will and a few of the men to guard the gate for the night. It was unlikely the Shire Reeve would be here immediately. He would have to gather warrants and organize his posse. And we didn't think he'd risk a night assault, not with every man in Sherwood carrying a longbow.

Robard's entreaty that I teach him to read had humbled me. His concern was genuine, and it was a hard thing for him to ask. I promised to have him reading in no time and in truth believed he would be a quick study. In fact I had already given him his first lesson, scratching out his name in the dirt of the courtyard, showing him the letters and the sounds they made. Later in the evening

I spotted him clandestinely practicing beside the fire while he enjoyed the company of his people, scratching away at the dirt with an arrow while the conversation went on around him.

When the meal was over, the talk continued, and I took leave to walk around the grounds and stretch my legs. Little John followed me.

"Something on your mind, lad?" he asked.

"Yes. And his name is William Wendenal. He will be here shortly, and in force. Robard and I locked him in his own jail and freed all of his prisoners. He can't let such a thing pass unanswered."

"For certain he will not," Little John agreed, glancing back at the happy revelers around the fire. "It's probably right and proper to let them enjoy their evening, but tomorrow we'd best prepare for a fight."

Yet another plan, I thought. When and if I ever delivered the Grail to Rosslyn, I hoped to move to a country where plans were never required.

"John, you served in the army. What do you see here? What advantages do we have over this Shire Reeve?" I asked.

He was quiet for a moment, thinking. "We've got at least twelve good men: Will and his bunch plus what hands were left here helping Mistress Hode. They all know the longbow; it's second nature to them. It keeps a man on horseback at a distance. I can make more points on the forge and anvil in the barn, so we're in good shape there. But if the reeve and his men get in close, if we must fight hand to hand, it won't go as well. We'll be outnumbered and no match for their swords and axes. Not to mention they'll probably have crossbows as well."

I nodded. The crossbows didn't bother me as much. They couldn't be spanned on horseback, and in a pitched battle, men with longbows could fire nearly twenty times for every shot from a crossbowman. What I worried over most were Will and his "Merry Men." Roaming the forest as bandits and preying on unsuspecting victims was one thing, but taking on trained, equipped and mounted fighters was another. For a moment I felt just as I had on the walls of Montségur, wishing I had Sir Thomas and a regimento of Templars at my side.

Then an image came to me. I remembered yesterday as we had ridden hard through Sherwood for Robard's home. We had stopped at the spring and Allan Aidale had climbed the tree to retrieve the cache of arrows. Robard, Will, Allan and the others were at home here in the woods. They used the forest for food and shelter and anything else they needed. There was our advantage. We couldn't stand toe-to-toe with the Shire Reeve in a straight-up fight. But we could certainly use the forest against him.

"What are you thinking?" Little John asked.

"I'm thinking about a hollow tree," I said. When I told him my plan, he smiled and clapped me on the shoulder.

"Tomorrow, then," he said as he sauntered off to the barn to sleep. We would need to rise early to implement my plan, and we all needed rest.

The next morning, the wind rose out of the west, and it had grown colder. When I stepped out of the house, the breeze bit into me. But I thought of something Brother Rupert had always said: "Sauce for the goose is sauce for the gander," meaning if we were going to be cold and miserable while the weather turned, so would the Shire Reeve and his men. If I had to bet, I would wager Robard and the people of Sherwood were much more able to tolerate the cold than Wendenal and his men. One more thing we might take advantage of.

Pottage simmered over the cook fire, and Will, Robard and the rest of the men stood about, looking like they had too much to do but no idea where to start. The first order was to prepare our defenses and choose the ground on which we would fight.

"Good morning, Tristan," Robard said. "Fine morning to each of you," he said to those assembled by the fire. "You know what happened to me in Nottingham. I went after Wendenal because I consider him a murderer. He can say he's only upholding the law, but there's no peace given to one who takes what isn't his in the name of an unjust law. There's going to be trouble, likely a fight or two before it's done. So if you've no stomach for it, leave now. If not, stay, but only if you're committed to standing with me."

Robard waited a moment, watching the eyes of everyone around him. There were new men at the fire this morning, and I was buoyed temporarily by the fact that they had answered their thane's call. They had heard the news of Robard's return, and his appearance had given them hope. They stood straight and strong, just like Will and Allan had. No one shirked or walked away but all stared back at him with clear eyes and pure hearts.

"Good. Most of you have met my friends, Tristan and Maryam. I've traveled far with both of them, and we've seen our share of scraps. Us and that yellow dog there," he said, smiling and pointing at Angel, who stood and wagged her tail at the attention.

"During the time I fought with the Lionheart—" He stopped and spat into the fire.

"Robin boy! Have you no manners!?" Mistress Hode said, whacking him on the arm.

"Sorry, Mother, but just the very mention of his name raises the bile in my throat. And every day there, I only wanted to come back here. To work our land, tend the soil, hunt in our forest and live out my life the way my father did and his father and every Hode before them. Tristan and Maryam were with me every step of the way home, and there's no finer folk anywhere. So what I'm telling each of you is this: As far as me and my mother are concerned, they're Hodes. If they speak, it's as if I said the words myself. My father was the thane before me, and it falls to me. I have made this so. If any of you see this as a problem, off with you now and no hard feelings."

Still no one moved.

"Good. I knew I could count on you. It looks to be a long, hard winter before this is over, but I promise you there are better days ahead. If I know anything, it's that Tristan here has an idea of how to handle William of Wendenal. So I say to you, listen to what he has to say and then let's get to work."

Robard shrugged at me. And I told them my plan.

25

 e needed two things to happen. First we needed a "rabbit" for Wendenal to chase, something that would lure him to the ground of our choosing. I sent riders out to scout and locate his force. Once they found him, I told them to make sure they were followed. Keep out of reach, but let Wendenal and his men see they were there and do whatever they could to get him to pursue them.

I had no idea how many bailiffs he would bring. Will estimated he could probably raise fifty from Nottingham alone, more if he drafted men from neighboring shires. Not being certain, we made plans for a large force to assault the Hode manor.

We worked with desperation to get ready. Not knowing when the Shire Reeve might show up made everyone nervous, and they threw their anxiety into their tasks. The scouts returned for fresh horses in the late afternoon and reported no sightings of men headed our way. We had made good use of the time, and by then we had most everything in place.

The next morning was cold again, with frost on the ground. The sky was dull and cloudy.

Robard bade everyone to attend to his weapons. Bowstrings were replaced and wallets filled with arrows. There was tension in the air as the threat of attack floated through the forest like an invisible beast.

At midday, Wendenal took the bait. Will's riders, a tall, rangy fellow everyone called Cutter and his companion, Clarence, a smaller version of Tuck, rode hastily into the yard. I heard the sound of Little John's hammer striking the anvil, and Robard gave a shout for everyone to assemble.

"He's coming, Master Hode," Cutter said. "He can't be more than a league behind us."

"Good work. It's time, everyone! To your places!" Robard shouted. The farm and yard became a flurry of activity as Will Scarlet and his bowmen took their wallets and melted into the trees. Little John and Brother Tuck also had roles to play, and they moved off to their spots. Robard and I had horses saddled and waiting and were about to be on our way when Maryam called out to him.

"Are you sure I can't come with you?" she asked.

He took her hands in his as she stood by the fire next to Mistress Hode.

"I would have you at my side if I were fighting the devil himself. But if this goes wrong, I need you here to protect my mother. I don't ask it lightly," he said.

"I know. And it's probably best I stay here. This *is* one of Tristan's plans, and it's likely to go wrong," she said, smirking. "Don't worry, Robard, I promise you the Shire Reeve of Nottingham will not lay a finger on your dear mother." She put a protective arm around Mistress Hode, who beamed. She and Maryam had become nearly inseparable since we arrived.

"You do know I can hear you, don't you?" I asked.

Robard laughed, gave Maryam a quick kiss on the cheek and vaulted onto his horse. Angel jumped up from where she had been sitting at Maryam's feet, ready to follow us, but I bade her stay with Maryam. She whined at first but complied. We slapped the reins and turned our mounts down the lane. I was riding Charlemagne, and Robard stared at me in mock concern.

"Are you sure you don't want a faster horse?" he sneered. "You may need it."

"No. Charlemagne and I have history. Besides, the Shire Reeve needs to believe you are a simple farmer and I am an inexperienced squire. Having me riding a plow horse is an element of my plan," I said, which was a complete and utter lie. Charlemagne was calm and steady, and it settled my nerves to ride him.

"Sure it is," Robard said. We rode quietly for a few moments. "You do realize this isn't likely to work."

"True, but we've done ourselves proud till now, haven't we?" I replied.

Robard muttered under his breath, but I only caught the words *barely* and *by the grace of God.*

As we rode down the lane to confront yet another enemy, the tall trees were majestic against the winter sky and helped cut the wind. The horses' breath came in great billowing gasps of fog. Reaching the gate, we stopped and waited. For several minutes we stood in silence, our anticipation growing.

"You don't suppose he gave up, do you?" Robard asked.

"Do men like that ever give up?" I countered.

"True," he said.

The woods were silent. The only sound was the occasional

crack and moan of limbs as the wind moved through the trees. Then, off in the distance, came the sound of men on horseback. They were moving slowly and with deliberation, but the creak of leather and the sound of hoofbeats were unmistakable.

I drew my sword and held it across the pommel of my saddle. Robard nocked an arrow in his longbow, holding it ready in his left hand with the reins in his right. Charlemagne snorted and blew, and Robard's horse nickered as they smelled the approaching column.

The men finally appeared through the trees: William Wendenal riding at the head of twenty-four bailiffs. I offered up a silent prayer at his arrogance believing so small a force would be adequate against us. He was perhaps half a league away when he spotted us and his posture changed. Sitting up in his saddle, he spurred his stallion and called his men forward. In moments, the column pulled to a halt twenty yards in front of us.

The bailiffs were well armed with swords and battle-axes but no longbows I could see, nor did they carry crossbows. Most of them wore leather tunics and riding breeches, but there was no visible armor or mail. Robard's fingers anxiously worked the grip of his longbow. It appeared Wendenal had had little time to equip his men, or he was expecting us to give up without a fight.

"Steady," I said quietly. "Let's hear what he has to say."

"By order of the King and his sovereign minister Prince John, you, Robard Hode, and you, Tristan of St. Alban's, are under arrest!" He reached into the fold of his tunic and removed a small rolled parchment. "I hold a duly drawn warrant stating same."

"Well, that settles it," I said sarcastically.

"If you've come to arrest me, I'd advise you to turn around

right now and ride back to Nottingham and never return. This is Hode land you're on, and if you intend to remove me from it, I give you fair warning you'll need far more than a slip of parchment," Robard proclaimed.

"You willfully disobey a direct and lawfully given command from a duly sworn officer of the King?" William Wendenal asked. There was a slight flicker of concern in his features. He seldom saw resistance. He was used to the power of his office, but we had humiliated the man in Nottingham, locking him in his own jail. He could not let it pass, yet he clearly expected that this show of force would bring us to our knees.

"I disobey it as willfully as I am able. I know what justice is, Shire Reeve, and what you *serve* is not it!" Robard said.

"Then you leave me no choice but to use force to subdue you," Wendenal replied.

"I expect that's true," Robard said. "In fact I was counting on it!"

And with those words he raised his bow, took aim at the Shire Reeve and fired. As we intended, his shot went wide and landed in the ground a few yards past Wendenal's mount. We turned our horses quickly and spurred them back in the direction we'd come. A quick glance over my shoulder showed Wendenal waving his arms and ordering his men forward.

Our hoofbeats pounded like thunder in my ears, and we made sure we stayed far enough ahead of Wendenal and his men. If my plan worked, we would greatly diminish his desire for a pitched battle. As we rode, we passed the first marker, a bit of red cloth I'd tied to a tree close to the lane.

"Now!" I shouted, and above the noise of our horses there

was a loud thunk as an ax bit into wood. The day before, we had chopped down a good-size tree, fastened ropes to both ends and hoisted it high into the treetops and tied it off. A rope at its center was tied to a tree across the lane, creating a giant pendulum when it was released. The log was hidden from view, and as the bailiffs rode after Wendenal, the rope holding it in place was cut and it swung down in a vicious arc, hitting the rear of the column and driving six of the bailiffs from their saddles.

Wendenal, riding hard after us, didn't even realize he had just lost one quarter of his force.

"Come on, you worthless snake!" Robard shouted at Wendenal, turning in the saddle to send another arrow in his direction. He had no intention of shooting the Shire Reeve, but wanted to make sure he kept pursuing us.

One hundred yards farther up the lane we passed the next marker. Another shout and two of Will's men on one side of the lane pulled on a large rope that had been hidden on the ground by dead leaves and grass. It rose up in a flash, anchored to another trunk across the lane. They quickly spun it around a tree to hold it in place, and this time the bailiffs at the head of the column were lifted right off their horses. Four riders went down hard. Behind them, the other mounted men reined up, their horses spooked and confused by the falling bodies and rearing horses in front of them.

"Now!" I shouted again, and this time a large net we had woven from rope and hidden beneath a thin layer of soil in the lane was hoisted into place behind the column. It was quickly tied off to two sturdy trees by Tuck and Little John, cutting the remaining dozen horsemen off from retreat. A hail of arrows from the trees kept them penned in.

Robard and I reined to a halt, turning our mounts to face the still-oncoming Wendenal.

"End this, Shire Reeve!" Robard commanded as Wendenal halted his horse a few yards away from us. "Before your men are injured further. We ask nothing more than that you leave us be. Go while you can, and forget about ever trying to take Hode land."

Wendenal glanced behind him at the confusion his bailiffs had suddenly found themselves in.

"Forward!" he shouted. "Take these men into custody! I order you!"

But Will, Allan and the other bowmen, hidden high above us in the trees, kept the fourteen remaining able-bodied bailiffs from taking even three steps.

Enraged, Wendenal gave the command to attack again, and another brace of arrows inched ever closer to his men. They were frightened. Every sensible man who had ever been in a fight feared archers, and here arrows were appearing as if by magic. I smiled.

"You can't win here, Wendenal," Robard said. "Leave, before it gets worse."

For a moment it occurred to me that I might have misjudged the man. He was undeterred and with a shout pulled his own sword, holding it high and spurring his horse toward Robard. With an almost unnatural calmness, Robard leapt from his horse. He calmly drew an arrow and fired. It whizzed through the air, striking Wendenal in the forearm. He screamed and dropped his sword, tumbling from his horse.

Moaning in agony and staring wild-eyed at the arrow sticking out of his arm, the Shire Reeve managed to stagger to his knees. Robard dismounted and slowly walked to him, kicking his sword away. Wendenal tried to stand but the pain was too much.

Robard pulled another shaft and nocked it in his bow.

"Robard!" I shouted. "He's defenseless!"

Robard drew and pointed the arrow directly at the center of Wendenal's chest. Despite grimacing in pain, he did not flinch or beg for his life. We have beaten him today, I thought, but this is not over.

"You are lucky, Shire Reeve, my friend Tristan of St. Alban's is here to guide my conscience, for were he not, I would dispatch you now and think nothing of it. Here is what is going to happen. You have trespassed on Hode property. You have come here uninvited—"

"You are a criminal!" Wendenal shouted. "I have a duly sworn warrant—"

"I don't care a sow's ear for your warrant, you miserable steaming pile of polecat dung. You are a tyrant and a bully. You and your men will walk out of Sherwood Forest. Your weapons and horses will be left behind as compensation for the transgressions you have committed against the people of Sherwood. Order your men to drop their swords, take your wounded and be gone. And do not come back."

"I'll be back," Wendenal sneered. "Don't you worry, Hode! Your life is forfeit! And yours too, squire. I'll bring a hundred men next time, two hundred if I need to. Do you really think your pitiful little band of peasants can stand against me?"

Robard said nothing, his bow still drawn, and for a moment I thought his resolve might weaken and he would let the arrow go. Then I was distracted by noise and movement, first to my right, then to my left. Men were moving through the woods, and for an instant I worried we had been outflanked. Somehow Wendenal had tricked us.

But through the trees came the people of Sherwood. I recognized many of their faces as those we had freed from the jail in Nottingham. They were dressed like Will and his men, and they had brought their families as well. Each of them carried some type of weapon: old swords, crossbows or longbows, a few with pitchforks and axes. They took up positions on either side of the lane, flanking the Shire Reeve and his bailiffs.

"Robard," I said quietly.

"I see them," he said. "Do you, Wendenal?"

The Shire Reeve held our gaze as more and more people poured out of the woods lining the lane. Cold resignation colored his face.

"Master Hode," one of the men from the jail called out to him. "We thought you might have some trouble, and after what you told us in Nottingham, well, we talked and decided that if you're ready to stand up for what is right, we are too. We're with you, Thane Hode!" There was a resounding cheer from the assembled people.

Robard smiled and lowered his bow, quickly slipping the arrow back into his wallet.

"There's your answer, Shire Reeve. You don't face just one. Here in Sherwood Forest you face an army of free men. Now do as I said. Gather up your bailiffs and get off my land. It's a long walk back to Nottingham. Will Scarlet!" he hollered out. "Make sure our uninvited guests find their way off the property."

Will shinnied gleefully down the tree where he had been hiding. "Aye, lad. I'll see to it."

"I'll be back, Hode!" The Shire Reeve spat out the words. "Don't think this is over."

"I don't think any such thing. And if it's more you want, come ahead. We'll be waiting. But for today, it's over right enough."

Robard turned on his heel and leapt up onto his horse. With a smile and a wink, he rode back up the lane and left William Wendenal kneeling in the dust, still gingerly holding his wounded arm. I followed Robard as the cheers of the people of Sherwood rang through the air.

26

ut Rob," Mistress Hode pleaded. "I still don't understand. You just came back to me. Why is it you must leave again? It's almost Yule, Rob! Your people need you here. What if that vicious Shire Reeve returns? What then?"

"Mother," Robard said calmly. "I don't know how else to explain it to you. There's something I must do. Tristan is on an important journey, and Maryam and I promised to see it through to the end. I can't go back on my word."

"Mistress Hode," I said quietly. She glanced at me with tear-filled eyes, which immediately made me feel selfish and ungrateful for the hospitality she had provided us. "I don't think you'll have any trouble with the reeve. We gave him a lot to think about yesterday, and I'm sure we'll be back long before he strikes again. Besides, Tuck and Little John will look after things. They know what to do." In truth, I had no idea if we would ever return, but I hoped to make her feel better.

Maryam and I sat on horseback as Robard held his mother gently, his big hands on her shoulders. Tears formed in her eyes and rolled down her cheeks, and the guilt I felt cannot be described.

The days after our "victory" over Wendenal had been joyous and filled with laughter and celebration. There was music and dancing, and each of the families from the surrounding countryside brought whatever food they had to share with everyone. Will and his men took to the woods and brought back deer and boar, and great feasts were prepared. They built huge fires and sang songs through the night. There were impromptu wrestling matches, with Little John taking on and defeating all who dared challenge him. Tall tales were told by everyone, and the overall feeling was one of happiness and peace, however temporary it might be.

Robard and Little John drank a great amount of ale, and before the night was over, they were sitting by the fire, singing at the top of their lungs, arms around each other, like long-lost brothers. The people of Sherwood who had given us aid when we needed it most had suffered much these last few months, and Robard and his mother saw to it that everyone at least had a full belly.

In gratitude, many of the men pitched in, helping Robard repair his buildings and fences, and with so many extra hands, the Hode place was quickly looking presentable again. And Robard smartly did not let his defeat of the Shire Reeve go to his head.

He explained to all the people of Sherwood what we had seen at Montségur and how the Cathars had used a horn to signal the approach of trouble. In the following week we built observation towers throughout Sherwood. Little John was able to fashion a cow horn at each station that could be sounded as a warning of the approach of any force. Everyone throughout the forest was instructed to head for the Hode house if the horn sounded three short blasts.

But as we worked, I worried. William Wendenal would be duty bound to report what had happened to his superiors. And in my mind, once word reached the court of Prince John, Sir Hugh would undoubtedly learn of our whereabouts. This would place everyone here in even greater danger. Sir Hugh would come with as many Templars as he could raise, and they would not be so easy to defeat as a few untrained or inexperienced bailiffs.

I could not be here when Sir Hugh arrived and risk danger to any of Robard's people. But when I told Robard and Maryam I intended to travel on to Rosslyn alone, they would have none of it. I knew better than to try to sneak away: they would just follow me. So we decided to leave together. The hard part was explaining it to Robard's mother and Tuck.

Tuck had become a hero to the people of Sherwood. Because he was in his monk's robes, they treated him like a fully ordained priest, even though he could never deliver a Mass or hear a confession. With his potions and herbs, he treated the sick and infirm, and he became their priest in spirit. Some even called him Father Tuck.

When I had said good-bye to him, I pointed to the three of us and made a walking motion with my fingers. I held my hands far apart, indicating I would be gone for a while. I pointed to Mistress Hode and tapped his chest, meaning he should stay with and look out for her. He nodded and clicked and cradled my face in his gentle hands before giving me an enormous hug. Then he saddled Charlemagne and provided us with some cloth bags full of food, potions, cooking utensils and other things we would need.

After Robard swore on his father's name he would return, his mother finally agreed to let him go. She shook her finger at me.

"You're a fine young lad, Tristan of St. Alban's, and I don't know what duty it is what draws you up among the Scots—a horrible people, I might add. But whatever it is, you make sure you bring my Robard back to me in one piece, do you hear?"

"Yes, Mistress Hode, I promise," I said. Without another word she left us quickly and disappeared inside the house.

As luck would have it, Little John had traveled to Scotland and knew some of the land. On an old piece of parchment, he was able to draw us a crude map. "Rosslyn lies along River Esk, south of Edinborough. Pass around Leeds—I expect you'll find lots of troops and Templars billeted there—and head north. If you find the River Esk, you'll find Rosslyn, right enough. But lad, it's just a tiny hamlet. What takes you there?"

I hemmed and hawed, not knowing what to tell John, and though I trusted him, I would not tell him of the Grail. No need to place his life in danger. He finally held up a hand before I could stammer out a reply. "Don't bother explaining, Tristan. Not my business anyway. But one more thing: watch out for the clans," he said.

"Clans?" I asked.

"Aye. The Scots all belong to different clans and most of 'em don't like each other much. My mother is Scottish, and they nearly cast her out for marrying an Englishman. They brawl amongst themselves like two badgers in a sack. Mean they are, and some of the fiercest fighters you'll ever see. If they ever got a mind to stick together, they'd push the English right off our mortal soil and into the ocean. But they can't stop squabbling amongst themselves most of the time. So be careful who you talk to or make friends with, because every friend you make in Scotland makes you an enemy of someone else."

Wonderful news, I thought. Thank you again, Sir Thomas, for this duty. How many more ways would I find to make enemies?

"John Little," Robard said, stepping forward. "I thank you for your help. I'm grateful to you for protecting my home and family while I'm gone. I will be in your debt forever."

Little John didn't hesitate. He stuck out his hand, and he and Robard shook heartily. "Well, you still do owe me two crosslets for crossing my bridge. But I'm honored to be asked. Don't worry. I know Will Scarlet is used to running things, and I'll make sure he believes he still is. But I'll keep an eye out till you get back."

Robard mounted his horse and the three of us were ready to leave. The Grail was safe in my satchel and Angel stood nearby, her tail wagging in anticipation of a new adventure.

"John," I said. "One more favor. Two days hence, I want you to send a few men into Nottingham. Don't let them get too close to the Shire Reeve, but have them visit the taverns and the marketplace and talk about what happened here. Have them let slip that we've headed north toward Scotland. I want word to get back to Wendenal that we've left, and hope it will keep Sir Hugh away from Sherwood. I don't think Wendenal is ready to launch another assault even if he believes we're gone. He realizes all the people are against him. He's going to have to wait awhile, to plan and gather his forces. But we need to get Sir Hugh to chase *us* so he doesn't threaten any of you."

Little John nodded his giant head. "Not to worry. I know what to do and I'll see it's done. If Sir Hugh shows up in these parts, we'll make certain he takes off after you long before he gets to Sherwood. But are you sure it's what you want?"

"Yes, it is." I nodded. With a little salute, I kicked Charlemagne gently in the sides and lumbered forward toward the tree-lined lane leading away from Robard's home. Robard and Maryam waved good-bye to everyone and their horses loped along beside me. Angel trotted briskly in front of us, her tail wagging and barking excitedly. She sniffed the ground and darted to and fro as we galloped up the lane. We passed beneath the wooden Hode sign and turned our horses quickly north.

It was time to bring an end to this.

27

 he closer we drew to Scotland, the more I worried over Sir Hugh's whereabouts. It was just a tingle along my neck, but I felt as if he were closing in. As we traveled, the winter deepened, and each night it became necessary to build a fire or risk freezing. I would have preferred to stay at inns or even seek shelter from farmers in their barns along the way, but doing so would make it easier for him to find us.

I fretted and fussed a great deal on the trip, second-guessing myself at every turn. Each night I would stare into the fire for hours, trying to determine Sir Hugh's next move. Where would he strike? How would I complete my mission while preventing him from wreaking havoc on my friends and their families? I could think of no easy answer, save what Robard and Maryam had already determined. He would not stop his quest for the Grail until his life was ended.

As Robard did in France, he rode apart from us during the day. For his mount, he had chosen a fleet roan gelding with great stamina, so each day he scouted, ranging far ahead, then circling back to check our rear, making sure our enemies did not take us by surprise.

He and Maryam were much more relaxed on the trip than I was. Before we left Hode land, Robard had given Maryam her own longbow and wallet of arrows, and when he returned each evening from his scout, he gave her shooting lessons. Her bow was a smaller version of his, and if I was any judge, she was becoming quite adept with it. Daggers and a longbow: now she was doubly lethal. Robard explained that it would take time to develop the muscles in her upper body to fully draw the bow, but before long she was easily striking tree trunks from forty and fifty paces away.

We also found time to continue Robard's lessons, scratching words in the dirt near the fire each night, practicing over and over again. He quickly mastered his name, the alphabet and a few simple words and phrases. And the farther along we went, the more he continued to grasp.

One night Robard returned to our camp with a rolled piece of parchment and a big smile on his face. He strode happily to me, and beamed as I studied it:

WANTED

Dead or alive,
Robard Hode, late of Sherwood Forest,
for crimes against the King.
Reward offered by William Wendenal,
Shire Reeve of Nottingham.

I looked at his expression quizzically.

"I recognized the words *Robard Hode* and *Sherwood Forest*," he said. Ah, that was why he was smiling. "But what does the rest say?" he asked.

"It says you are wanted for crimes against the King and that a reward is being offered by William Wendenal," I said.

"Excellent! A price on my head!" he exclaimed, even happier than before. "I found it on a signpost in a village I rode through this morning. Does it say how much I'm worth?"

"Alas, no, it is not specific as to your value," I replied.

"How can you joke about this?" Maryam exclaimed, shaking her head. "This isn't funny."

"It most certainly is," Robard said. "If there's to be a price on my head, I want to make sure I'm not being undersold. Besides," he said, handing her the parchment so she could read it for herself, "aren't you proud of the fact that I could read well enough to recognize my own death warrant?"

Maryam shook her head in exasperation. "Yes, Robard, I'm very proud of you. But I'd still be if you couldn't read a word. This is nothing to make light of. All this time, as we've traveled together, you've wanted nothing more than to go home to your family. And after seeing your land and the people, I understand why you were so eager. But this . . ." She shook the parchment at him. "This changes everything! You're not safe here. You've made an enemy of the Shire Reeve, and with times being so desperate, many will turn against you at the thought of a reward and . . ."

Robard quickly drew an arrow from his wallet and let it fly. It plunked into a tree a short distance away. He had moved so quickly,

I had had no time to react and at first thought we were under attack. I scrambled to draw my sword and Maryam crouched, reaching for her daggers.

"That is what I think of William Wendenal and his price on my head. Both of you calm down. The Shire Reeve is not to be feared. He revealed his true colors back in Sherwood. He is a coward, and as for his reward he can kiss my—"

"Robard!" Maryam exclaimed.

"What?" he asked, feigning ignorance.

With an exasperated sigh, Maryam stormed off into the woods. Angel apparently took her side and trotted along beside her.

"Why is she so upset?" he asked me.

"You're asking me?" I said. "How many times must I remind you I grew up in a monastery? Perhaps she feels you're being reckless, refusing to acknowledge how dangerous your life has become. You realize once this is over and you return to Sherwood, it will not be peaceful. Not as long as William Wendenal is there."

Robard plopped down on a log next to the fire. "Feh," he said, kicking at one of the flaming timbers with his boot. "Wendenal doesn't worry me."

We let the conversation drop, and before long Maryam returned from her sojourn to the forest and we all fell into a fitful sleep, with each of us taking turns standing watch.

The next morning, we ate a light breakfast from the bag of food Tuck had sent along with us and then Robard rode off, as was his custom.

Later in the day, we skirted the city of Leeds and kept heading north. The countryside became more remote and uncultivated, with dense forest and underbrush, and it was often difficult to find a clear trail. We crossed back and forth trying to make decent time, but the landscape did not cooperate.

A few days later we finally pushed past the city of Gateshead and made better time along the coast. Now that we were firmly inside Scottish boundaries, Little John's words came back to me and I worried about the clans. Each morning as Robard prepared to depart on his scout, I begged him not to engage in any conflict with anyone. The last thing we needed was angry Scotsmen chasing us in addition to the King's Guards and whatever Templars Sir Hugh had enlisted. He promised he wouldn't, and for several days he spoke to no one.

One night he returned to our camp and asked to see the crude map Little John had drawn for us.

"What was the name of the river leading to Rosslyn?" he asked.

"The River Esk," I replied. "Why?"

"I found it," he said. "There is a small hamlet not far north of here, and I inquired from a smith if he knew the river. Told him I had cousins lived along it, south of Edinborough. He wasn't a friendly chap. Scotsmen aren't free with the talk. But I dragged the location out of him, and sure enough rode off and found it."

We were almost there. As we lighted a fire that evening and sat by it talking amongst ourselves, I pondered our next moves. We should reach Rosslyn tomorrow, and I felt excitement and nervousness all at once. After months of desperate travel, the end of my journey was near.

As the fire dimmed, we all grew quiet and I wondered if Maryam and Robard were thinking the same thoughts as I.

Then a low growl sounded in Angel's throat and she stood up. We were shocked to see our camp surrounded by ten mounted men. They all wore kilts and carried large battle-axes, swords and various other instruments for killing and maiming.

We did not have to worry about finding the Scots. They had found us.

28

he three of us stood back to back, our weapons in our hands. Angel growled and barked and stood in front of me. The men said nothing and their horses stood stock-still. Their faces were painted in an odd assortment of colors. One of them did not brandish a weapon and nudged his horse forward.

"Guid evenin' tae yoo," he said.

"What did he say?" Robard whispered to me.

"I'm not sure. I think he said he was going to eat us," I answered back.

"What?" Robard cried.

"I think he said 'good evening,'" Maryam offered.

"I thought he said 'good eating,'" I replied.

The man on horseback watched us talk amongst ourselves for a moment.

"Yur oan McCullen land," he said.

"What did he say now?" Robard asked.

"Something about someone named McCullen and his hand," I said.

"No, he said he's with McCullen's band. They look like they're just back from a fight or about to leave for one," Maryam said.

"Tristan, you better see if you can talk us out of this," Robard said.

"Me? Why me?"

"You chose this campsite—this is your fault," he said. "Besides, you gave me specific instructions not to talk to any Scots."

"What? No, it was Maryam who found it, not me," I said.

The man, who I assumed was their leader since he did the talking, nudged his horse a little closer to us. With the firelight, I could see him more clearly, and immediately wished I could not. Scars lined his face like a brush pile, and he had them everywhere. Over both eyes, along his chin and one in particular that started by his left ear, traveled down his cheek and disappeared into the collar of his cloak.

"Wha' brings ye oot haur?" he asked.

"Hello, my name is Tristan. May I ask your name?"

The man tilted his head back and looked at me as if he were trying to focus. I gripped the hilt of my sword tightly. I wondered if I had violated some ancient Scottish custom by requesting his name. Knowing my luck I had just challenged him to a duel.

The man grunted, "A'am th' Earl a' McCullen. Yur oan mah lain." He was an Earl with a hand in the air? Something about his hand?

Looking up at the man and his nine mounted companions, I decided diplomacy was our only option. Slowly and with great deliberation, I retuned my sword to its scabbard and held my hands up in front of me.

"Tristan!" Robard said through gritted teeth. "What are you doing? Have you gone mad?"

"We're not going to fight our way out of this one, Robard. I'm wondering if we aren't on his land and he's asking me for an explanation of why we're trespassing," I said.

"If we have trespassed here, we are sorry and we will quickly be on our way," I said.

He looked down on me from his horse and then dismounted slowly, never taking his eyes off the three of us. Slowly he strode toward me until he was an arm's length away. He was taller than I was, by a half foot at least, and he looked even more frightening close up.

"That's a braw lookin' sword thaur," he said. He pointed to Sir Thomas' battle sword on my back. It was impossible for me to divine his meaning. Did he want the sword? Was he going to steal it from me?

I held up my left hand and very slowly, using just the tips of my fingers, pulled the sword free of the scabbard. It was so heavy I nearly dropped it, but I held on to it, grasped the blade with my right hand and held it out for him. He took it from me and inspected it closely.

"Urr ye Crusaders?" Then it came to me: he wanted to know if I was back from the war.

"Yes, yes!" I said, nodding vigorously. "We're back from Outremer." The word got his attention.

"Ootremer? Urr ye a Templar?"

"Yes, sir, I am of the Order but not a knight," I said, and then wondered if I had made a mistake. What if he considered the

Knights Templar to be his enemies?

"Beautiful blade," he said, returning the sword to me. "Urr ye hungry?"

I didn't know what to do or say. Without understanding him, I was afraid my next words could be my last if I said the wrong thing. To my immense relief he repeated himself and made a motion of spooning food into his mouth. Aha!

"Are we hungry? Yes, we are," I said, which was true, as we had not eaten yet.

The man gave a command and his men dismounted. From out of the shadows they emerged with several sacks and jugs that had been tied to their horses. I gave a nod to Robard and Maryam, and they lowered their weapons.

"I think they're going to feed us," I said.

"Are you sure they aren't going eat us?" Robard cracked.

"I'm reasonably certain they won't," I answered.

He knelt by the fire and watched as his men prepared the meal. In short order a flank of venison was roasting over the fire and they passed around a bag of bread. We each took a small piece.

"My name is Tristan," I said again, holding out my hand. The man took it and nearly crushed every bone in it with his grip.

"The Earl a' McCullen," he said. I finally figured out that he was the Earl of someplace called McCullen, which I assumed was a nearby estate or manor. Or maybe his name was McCullen. I couldn't be sure.

He broke off a small piece of bread and held it out to Angel, who still maintained her position between us. Her resolve melted on seeing the scrap of food in his hand. She inched forward and gulped down the bread. Then she allowed the man to scratch behind her ears.

"Whaur ye headin'?" the Earl asked. The more he talked, the better I could understand his thick Scottish brogue.

"We are traveling to Rosslyn," I said. His eyes went wide, and before I could speak, a small ax appeared out of his cloak, and he tossed it so quickly and effortlessly, I almost did not see it until it thudded into a tree ten feet away.

Apparently, I had said the wrong thing.

29

o one moved. The entire camp was silent. Maryam and Robard stood stock-still, afraid to reach for their weapons, their eyes wide. The Earl glared at me.

"Why urr ye ridin' tae Rosslyn?" he asked, the fingers of his right hand tickling the hilt of his sword, which hung at his side.

"Well . . . you see . . . we are going there to meet someone," I said.

"Who will ye meit thaur?"

Now I was truly unsure of what to do or say. I couldn't be sure, but it appeared that the Earl and his men had been raiding or fighting someone, maybe in northern England or perhaps another clan. When he understood we were Crusaders, he made some internal judgment and perhaps accepted us as kindred spirits. He was certainly no one to be trifled with, and I could not reveal my true mission, but a lie very close to the truth might work.

"I need to deliver a letter to Father William at a church there," I said.

"Faither William?" he asked.

I nodded yes and smiled, wanting to make sure the angry Scotsman knew I was his friend.

"Why urr ye seekin' Faither William?" he asked.

"I served with his brother in Outremer. I'm sorry to say, he was killed in battle. I'm taking his last words to Father William." It was all I could think of on the spot, and as soon as the words left my mouth, I realized he could easily discover my deception. What if he knew Father William didn't have a brother? Or he wanted to see the letter? Knowing my luck, he *was* Father William's brother.

"Oh, puir Faither William," he said. He bowed his head and closed his eyes and prayed silently for a moment, then crossed himself.

"In th' mornan' we'll tak' ye thaur," he said.

Robard and Maryam had relaxed, but we were all still wary.

"Did he just say 'there's a bell cow here'?" Robard asked.

"No, he said he'll take us to Rosslyn in the morning."

"Wonderful," said Maryam, not meaning it at all.

The Scots were excellent campfire cooks, and we listened to them laugh and tell stories of their exploits long into the night. We couldn't understand a word of what they were saying but were afraid to be impolite. From their laughter and antics, the tales were apparently funny and full of adventure. We'll never know. Then it was time for rest, and they all dropped where they sat and went to sleep.

"Should we try to leave?" Robard whispered.

"I don't think so. The Earl might be insulted. Let's try to get some sleep and worry about it in the morning," I said.

But I did not sleep. I half expected another clan to arrive and murder us all in our sleep. The horses the Earl and his men rode looked loaded with plunder, and someone must have been after them. Finally sleep overtook me and I remembered Little John's admonition: "For every friend you make in Scotland, you make an enemy of someone else."

I slept fitfully, waking every few minutes to keep an eye on my new "friends."

Something nudged me awake. I looked up to see a boot attached to a leg. Then I heard the words "It's mornan'. Gie up." What? It didn't make sense. Did someone say it was time for soup? It was not even dawn yet.

When I came fully awake, I found the boot belonged to the Earl. He repeated the words, and by now, I was awake enough to understand. He had said it was time to get up. We stood and found the Earl's men already mounted up and prepared to ride. Hastily gathering our belongings, we too were ready to depart in a few moments.

The Earl climbed up on his own horse, a large black stallion. "Rosslyn's tae th' north."

"He just said, 'Rosslyn is north,'" Robard said, delighted he had deciphered the Earl's announcement.

"I know. I heard him," I said. We followed along behind the Earl but ahead of his column of men.

"Do you think this is a good idea?" Maryam asked.

"No. Yes. I don't know. At first I thought not, but perhaps if he shows us the way to Rosslyn, we'll be less likely to run into any trouble with his countrymen," I said.

"Unless a bigger, meaner Scotsman with more men comes along," Robard said.

"Thank you for mentioning that, Robard," I replied sarcastically.

"I do what I am able," he said.

We rode through the countryside all morning, and unlike us, the Earl rode through towns and villages with little thought. No one appeared to pay us any attention, but we did stand out, and I worried Sir Hugh would learn of our presence before long.

Shortly after midday we forded the River Esk and climbed up a tall promontory that I later learned the locals called Rosslyn Glen. It was a beautiful spot, with rolling hills that must have been magnificently green in summer. The sound of rushing water made the forest and the earth around us sound as if it were alive, with its own pulse and beating heart.

In the middle of the small village of Rosslyn stood the spire of a church steeple. I hoped it was the Church of the Holy Redeemer that Sir Thomas had instructed me to find. My heart sprang for joy at the thought.

Then as fast as my hopes had risen, they were dashed. Hanging from the gate of the village hung a Templar banner, and a half dozen Templars guarded the entrance.

Sir Hugh was waiting.

ell, this truly ruins a fine day," Robard said, staring at the knights assembled below us. They were camped outside the town walls, with several tents and a cook fire blockading the village gate. Not far away their horses were hobbled and grazed quietly on the underbrush and grass.

The Earl and his men retreated a few paces out of sight of anyone watching from below.

They looked impatient to be on their way. Something told me the Earl was no longer on his lands and would likely find trouble with another clan if he delayed too long. He rode up beside me and offered his hand.

"Guid luck tae ye," he said. As far as we go. We shook hands and I winced as he squeezed my hand with a death grip. Then we watched him and his men melt away into the trees.

"Lovely people," Robard said.

"I expect it could have been worse," I said.

"Sure, after all, they could have eaten us. Now instead we get to face Sir Hugh and a brace of Templars." Robard often delighted in pointing out the many challenges of our situations.

"How does Sir Hugh keep finding us? How could he have known where you were headed?" Maryam asked as we returned to the top of the glen to study the town.

I couldn't answer, because in finding him already here, I had come to a horrible conclusion. Someone in Sir Thomas' inner circle must have been one of Hugh's spies.

"I don't know. When Sir Thomas entrusted the Grail to me, he spoke of a small circle of knights within the Order who knew of its existence. It had been their solemn duty to keep it safe. No one else, not even brother knights beyond those few, even knew it was real. But he must have suspected something or someone was unfaithful to their Code, or else he wouldn't have instructed me to give it to a priest and not a fellow Templar."

In truth, none of it mattered anymore. I would find Father William and do as Sir Thomas had ordered. Even if Sir Hugh had beaten us here, and even though it was a mystery how he was always able to stay a step ahead of us, it was time for this to be over.

"What now?" Robard asked.

"We wait until nightfall. I'll sneak into the city and try to find out as much as I can about these knights, and whether Sir Hugh is holding any hostages. If I can find Father William, I can sneak him out of town and he can decide what to do with the Grail."

"We won't allow you to go in alone," Robard said. But I ignored him.

It was approaching late afternoon. We found a copse of trees fed with a spring and watered the horses. The trees would keep us somewhat hidden, but I doubted Sir Hugh would be sending out scouts or setting pickets. He was waiting for me to come to him.

We spent anxious hours anticipating nightfall. Maryam sharpened her daggers on a stone, and Robard tended to his bow and inspected each of his shafts, and took the time to examine several bundles of arrows he had tied to the back of his saddle. I paced back and forth nervously while Angel slept.

"Why don't we just leave?" Robard finally suggested. "We can go back to Sherwood. You're both welcome to stay there as long as you like. Let Sir Hugh wait here until he grows old and feeble." Maryam smiled when Robard mentioned returning to Sherwood, and her expression told me that when this was over, going back to her home in Outremer was no longer first on her list of things to do. For some reason, her look reminded me of Celia, and I thought how I would almost rather be back in France, penned inside Montségur, than freezing in the woods of Scotland.

I shook my head. "I can't. Sir Thomas told me the Grail would be safe here. What if Sir Hugh is holding Father William against his will? What if he's murdered him? I can't just leave without knowing his fate."

"So you're going to go through with it?" Robard asked. "Try to sneak into the village after dark? Alone?"

"There's no moon tonight. I'll make my way in somehow and find out what has happened to Father William. If Sir Hugh is not holding him, I will try to persuade him to leave with me. If he is a hostage, I'll return here and plan our next move."

"You should let me go instead," Maryam said. "I'm stealthier than you are."

"You are, but you and Robard will likely need to rescue me when this plan fails," I joked.

After sundown, I made myself ready. While waiting I'd thought long and hard about my next moves.

"It's time," I said.

"Tristan," Robard said, "we should come with you."

I shook my head no and Robard let out an exasperated sigh.

"You've come a long way. And you want to finish this on your own. I understand that. Just be careful. If you don't succeed, if we are unable to rescue you, what should we do?"

"If I don't come back, you two return to Sherwood. Forget about trying to rescue me. You've both done more than enough. If you're right, Sir Hugh is waiting for us and it's me he wants. If I can find Father William, I'll try my best to sneak him out, but if I'm not back by morning, don't wait for me. Get out of here and get to safety."

"But Tristan," Robard said, "what about the Grail?"

"I've done everything I can do, Robard. Sir Hugh and I will end this now and the Grail will be safe, or I will die defending it. This has gone on long enough."

As I left my friends behind, I hoped they did not see in me what I felt then.

That if Sir Hugh waited for me in the town below, I might never see them again.

31

osslyn was likely the smallest village I had ever
seen that was completely enclosed by a wall.
It must have been because, as Little John said,
the Scots were fighting someone most of the
time and the wall had become a mandatory
means of defense. If Rosslyn were populated by people like Earl
McCullen, the wall made sense. Having seen the Earl and his men
up close, I could imagine them on either side of such a barrier,
attacking or defending.

It took some time for me to work my way down the hillside.
I had circled the entire village from the safety of the forest, looking for a way in or out. There was a rear gate, opening onto a road
leading to the north. Six knights guarded each entrance. There were
no men on the eastern or western walls I could see, but I had to
assume there were more inside the village, patrolling the streets or
watching the church. I counted to five hundred to make sure, but
no guards appeared on the parapets. Nor did the knights at each
gate ever circle the perimeter. With no one standing watch on the
walls, that could be my way in. Or it could be part of Sir Hugh's
plan to have intentionally left the battlements unguarded, hoping

to draw me in. Perhaps he lacked the resources to guard every entrance. Ultimately it didn't matter. I had to get inside.

The stone walls were approximately twelve feet tall. And that was my next obstacle. We had not brought any length of rope with us. I didn't think I could climb the walls unaided. I retreated into the woods and came upon a brush pile where a field had been cleared for planting. It lay fallow, but there were several saplings and lengths of timbers lining it in a crude fencerow filled with haphazardly stacked tree stumps. I found a limb about six inches in diameter and about fourteen feet long. Using my short sword I chopped away the branches, making a crude ladder. I was far enough removed from the gates and didn't think the knights would hear me. When I completed my alterations, I hoisted it up on my shoulder, delighted that it was light enough for me to carry.

I returned to the tree line facing the east wall. There was still no one in evidence on the parapets or the grounds below. Crouching as low to the ground as I could, I crept down the hill and toward the wall. It was an unwieldy gait, putting an excruciating strain on my wounded side, but I couldn't risk dragging the tree for the noise it would make.

With luck I reached the base of the wall and propped my scaling ladder against it at a slight angle. I ascended the crude steps, climbing carefully. Halfway up, one of the branches could not support my weight and cracked loudly when I stepped on it. I fell against the trunk and thought I might totter over to the ground, but managed to brace myself. I waited a moment, fearing the noise must have attracted someone, but no one came, so I climbed on.

When I reached the top, I pulled the limb up and over the parapet and laid it against the wall so it would be there if I needed it for my escape. A nearby ladder on the inner side took me down inside the town. I drew my sword and made my way to the side of the closest building. I smelled livestock; it must have been a stable or livery of some kind. From this vantage point, I peered down the road toward the center of the village. Here and there a few torches were lighted, and dim light came through the windows of a few buildings.

Instinct warned me to be cautious. I waited, counting to a thousand before I moved again. My goal was to reach the church, but along the way, I would check every direction for a trap.

I studied the street before me for a good while. And for as long as I dared, I took my time, carefully circling, darting from shadow to shadow and finding whatever cover I could, keeping the spire of the church as my vantage point, and watching for guards or knights or anyone who might be lying in wait for me. But there was nothing suspicious. If they were there, they had done a masterful job of hiding themselves.

Finally, I worked my way to the church. How I hoped for a sign, anything to positively identify that this was where I was supposed to be. Words painted on the door would have been extremely helpful: TRISTAN, PLEASE DELIVER THE GRAIL HERE. Darting from building to building, I encircled the church trying to learn all of the ways in or out. For such a small village it was a good-size structure, and my guess was that it was also a place of worship for many who lived outside the town walls. However, it appeared to have only a single front door.

Cautiously, and as furtively as I was able, I made my way to the shadows of the front door. Taking a last quick look behind me, I lifted up on the heavy wooden door handle and pushed, hoping there would be no squeak of alarm from the hinges. I opened it just far enough to slip through.

Looking at my drawn sword, I felt a tremendous surge of guilt for entering a house of the Lord with a weapon in my hand and malice in my heart. But I offered up a quick prayer asking God to forgive this transgression, as I hoped he had forgiven so many others of mine, and asked him to understand I was here to do his work and that the sword might be necessary. I also asked him if we could discuss it later, as I was very busy at the moment.

The vestibule of the church was quiet and empty, but light came from two oil lamps mounted on the walls on either side of the door leading to the chapel. Quickly running to the doorway, I peeked inside to find it deserted, save for a solitary figure in dark brown priest robes kneeling at an altar lighted by candles, lost in prayer. Still suspecting a trap, I hugged the wall of the chapel and made my way forward, sword at the ready.

I feared the worst. I was but a few feet away, but I could hear no prayers, nor any sound at all coming from the priest. When I was close enough to touch him, I spoke quietly.

"Excuse me, but might you be Father William?" I asked.

He gave no response. With my free hand I reached out to nudge him on the shoulder. When I did, he slumped forward, his body twisting and landing faceup on the altar.

I pushed back his cowl with the edge of my sword and gasped. A dead man stared up at me. His hands were bound together in front of him, locked in eternal prayer. I was too late. Father William was dead.

32

ir Hugh had killed another innocent, and I had failed to stop him. I spun around, expecting Sir Hugh and his men to suddenly appear, but the church was still deserted. I ran back up the aisle between the pews and cracked open the front door. There was no one in sight. Where was he? Why was he tormenting me? He had to realize I was here. Why would he not show himself?

I couldn't gather his reason for killing Father William and leaving his body in the church if he wasn't watching for me at all times. Had he grown sloppy? Did he think I was a fool who would blindly stumble into his trap anyway?

With a deep breath, I darted out of the church and across the square, and took shelter in an alley between rows of shops. The town was still quiet. I wondered if Sir Hugh had forced everyone out, leaving it easier to guard and control until I arrived. But it was unlikely he could evacuate an entire village of even this modest size, filled with testy Scots, with so few knights.

Following the alley to the next street, I kept my back to the wall and peered around the corner. I studied every doorway, rooftop and potential hiding place, but I could see nothing or no one in evidence. For a moment I wished Angel were with me, for her nose and hearing would have been a keen advantage.

Not willing to rush headlong into a trap, I took another circuitous route back to the wall where my scaling ladder lay hidden. Making sure no one was following or lying in wait to ambush me, I replaced the log against the wall and climbed over and down the other side. I had used up most of the night, and light was gathering in the east. It was going to be a bitterly cold day, but I hardly noticed the falling temperature.

As fast as I could, I worked my way back up to the camp where I had left Maryam and Robard. With Father William dead, I had no idea what to do with the Grail. But I would worry about it later. Getting away from here was my first priority.

When I reached the point where I could look down on the village, I was shocked to see that the knights guarding the entrance had vanished. All that remained were their tents and cook fires. Where had they gone?

As the sun rose, snowflakes drifted out of the sky. The wind picked up, and my face and hands grew cold. A feeling of dread came over me as I approached the copse of trees where I'd left Maryam and Robard. Where was Angel? She would have smelled me coming and should have burst to my side in greeting. Something was very, very wrong.

For a moment, the woods thickened and I thought perhaps I was lost. Then I heard a familiar snort and burst through a clump of underbrush to find Charlemagne tethered to a tree. He nickered at my approach and I patted him on the withers. He was saddled and ready to ride, but the bags of food Tuck had packed for us, as well as the bundle of arrows that I'd carried lashed to the back of my saddle, were gone.

Had Robard and Maryam taken my words to heart? Perhaps I had spent too much time in Rosslyn and they assumed I'd been captured, and had followed my instructions to escape. No. That couldn't be it. Robard and Maryam would never follow my instructions. They would have come to find me if they were able. Something must have spooked them. I was no tracker but would have to see if I could find where they had gone.

I climbed into the saddle and was about to spur Charlemagne away when I spotted one of Robard's arrows lying on the ground, just outside our camp. I could have easily missed it, but I stopped and studied it for a moment. It was not stuck in the ground, point first. It was lying flat, pointing to the south, back in the direction we had come the day before.

The arrow gave me pause. It might have accidentally fallen from one of the bundles they carried on their saddles. Or perhaps it had tumbled unexpectedly from their wallets as they mounted their horses.

But I was sure it hadn't. Robard treated his shafts like gold. He would not be so careless. The arrow was a signal. They had headed south.

I steered Charlemagne through the woods, and the sun was coming up, but the snow fell more heavily. I pulled my cowl up around my neck and rode on.

I approached the promontory we had climbed the day before where the River Esk ran below. The wind picked up and the snow stung my face, but as I drew closer to the high ridge, I spied a small group of figures on horseback in front of me. I reined Charlemagne to a halt a few paces away.

Before me Sir Hugh sat mounted in the center of a line of knights. On either side of him, still on their horses, were Robard and Maryam, with their hands bound behind their backs.

quire," Sir Hugh said hatefully.

"Sir Hugh. What brings you to these parts?" I struggled to keep my voice calm.

A vision of the crosses lining the lane at St. Alban's appeared in my mind. The image of poor Brother Tuck alone in the woods nearby, left without the only home he'd ever known. All of the horror visited on the world because of this vile, evil excuse for a man churned through me.

Robard and Maryam both looked crestfallen. I mouthed the word *Angel*, and Robard shrugged. He didn't know what had happened to her. Why had she not warned them of Sir Hugh's approach?

The mounted knights sat six to a side beside the prisoners. Some of them carried lances, and most held swords across the pommel of their saddles. They blockaded the path leading from the high ridge down to the river. There was no escape for me. This was the end.

And in truth, I was ready for it. Sir Thomas could ask no more of me. He had given me an order and I had followed it as best I could. I would not let Sir Hugh kill my friends. Not for anything. But I also would not give up without a fight.

"Where is it, boy?" Sir Hugh asked.

"Where is what?" I replied.

Sir Hugh drew his sword with blinding speed and held it out so it sat poised, just inches from Maryam's neck.

"Who dies first?" He smirked. God himself could not imagine how sick I was of his face. How I wished to crush it beneath my boot.

"Don't tell him, Tristan," Maryam said. "You can't let this swine—" Her words were cut off by Sir Hugh deftly slashing at her with his blade. A small cut opened on her neck. Maryam did not flinch, but Robard went mad. He shouted and tried to dismount his horse, and the knight next to him clubbed him hard across the face. Robard rocked back, nearly tumbling from the saddle, but remained upright, stunned but still cursing.

"Leave them alone, you miserable wretch," I said. I dropped Charlemagne's reins and grasped the strap of the satchel in my right hand. If ever I needed the power of the Grail, it was now. But there was no hum, no vibration or song that I had come to recognize in times of danger. Somewhere along the way I must have sinned, and God had deserted me.

Slowly and with great deliberation, I dismounted. Sir Hugh sat still on his horse, watching me intently, but with a small measure of confusion in his eyes.

"All right, Sir Hugh," I said as I removed Sir Thomas' battle sword from its familiar place across my back and tossed it aside. Never tearing my eyes from him, I drew my own sword. "Let's end this." I took my stance and waited.

Sir Hugh's eyes grew wide first in fascination, then amusement.

"Tristan, no!" Maryam shouted as Sir Hugh leapt from his horse.

The knights moved from their straight line facing me to form a crude circle around us, with two of them remaining beside Robard and Maryam. I never took my eyes off Sir Hugh, ignoring the wind and snow beating at my face. My hand gripped the hilt so tightly that I thought it would burst. Rage boiled in my stomach as I stared at Sir Hugh like a hawk might study a field mouse. Be ready, I told myself.

"This must be my lucky day," Sir Hugh taunted me. "I get to kill you, and your friends, *and* take the Grail." He tried to draw me in with feints and thrusts, but I was patient. I would not let him goad me into attacking him with blind rage.

"Tell me, squire," he said. "How does it feel to come all this way, to get so close only to fail? I find it quite humorous. Sir Thomas should have been more careful picking his squires."

"Are you hoping to talk me to death?" I asked. "Or are you going to fight?"

Sir Hugh's face turned crimson and he attacked with fury. He swung his sword in a vicious downward arc. His blade crashed into mine and sparks flew into the winter air as our blades locked together momentarily. The force of his blow nearly drove me to my knees, but I managed to push back and gain space between us.

Bad enough I was dueling a superior swordsman, but as the snow gathered at our feet, the ground was becoming wet and slippery. Sir Hugh lunged with the point of his sword coming straight at my chest. I pushed it to the side and dodged away.

"You can't win, squire," he sneered at me, plunging forward again. I blocked, but he was too strong, and his blade grazed my sword arm where it met the shoulder. I felt nothing for a brief second, and then pain raged through me. He laughed as blood

220

darkened my tunic. Some inner will prevented me from showing my anguish. He would get no satisfaction from me.

We traded blows and I swung savagely. I knew I should remain calm, but I was finding it more difficult to contain my rage. My swings rained down on Sir Hugh, but he easily parried every one.

Already my breath was coming in ragged gasps. We circled each other. Sir Hugh darted at me again and I danced out of the way, spinning around and slashing him across the arm of his empty hand.

He jumped back, looking down at the wound in shock.

"Apparently we both bleed, Sir Hugh," I said.

He came at me in a flurry of blows. All I could do was hold on to my sword with both hands, keeping it in front of me, trying to sweep his blade away. He cut me deeply on the left forearm, and I cried out this time. Then another slash nearly took me in the chest, but I jumped back just enough, and instead his sword sliced neatly through the strap on the satchel and it fell to the ground.

I struggled to get clear of it, afraid of stumbling. My arms were suddenly weak, and it was difficult to lift my sword. Maryam and Robard were yelling instructions to me, but I could not focus on what they were saying.

Sir Hugh stood perhaps six paces away from me, the satchel on the ground between us. He circled to my left and I countered, moving to his right. Despite the cold, I was sweating. I felt weak. He came at me again, and I was so exhausted that I could not lift my sword in time and he opened a vicious slash on my chest. He laughed, and then his foot kicked out at me, landing in my stomach, and I flew backward to the ground. I was down and barely able to struggle to my knees. Sweat poured into my eyes, and the whipping wind and snow made it difficult to see.

Sir Hugh appeared in front of me out of the snow with his sword raised over his head. I don't know where I found the strength, but as he whipped it downward, I lifted my sword over my head with both hands. His blade was blocked, but with a sickening crack my sword broke in two. I swung at him with the broken blade as I tried to stand, but Sir Hugh stepped well back out of reach.

Then as the wind blew fiercely across the hilltop, I spied Sir Thomas' sword on the ground a few feet away, nearly covered in snow. I dropped forward to my hands and knees and crawled toward it.

"Look at you! Crawling along the ground like an animal, knowing I have bested you. Though I'll give you some small measure of credit, squire," he said. "You're not quite the worthless, puny weakling you once were. In a few more years you may have become almost a worthy adversary. And what makes this so enjoyable for me, besides the fact that you are about to die, is how I managed to destroy everything in your life. You've been to St. Alban's, no doubt. You know I had it burned to the ground. Since I couldn't give a whit about Eleanor or her desires anymore, I'm just going to kill you. It doesn't even matter who you really are."

"Less talk, more fighting," I said wearily as I scrambled along the ground. But then I decided that if I could get him talking, he might grow careless. He did love to brag, and I needed only a few more feet to reach the sword.

"How did you know to come here?" I asked.

"Ha! You worthless fool! How did I find you in France? I have spies everywhere, especially within the Order. I hear and know everything! Sir Thomas thought he could keep the Grail from me.

He was more stupid than you. He never knew I was three steps ahead of him the entire time. It was no trouble at all to find the place he'd ordered you to go. You evaded me in Dover, but I knew you'd come here eventually. I only needed to wait."

I was almost there, just a few more feet. "You better learn to enjoy your own company, Sir Hugh. Kill us all and see what good it does you. Take the Grail. You'll never be able to keep it. You talk too much. You won't be able to resist telling someone what you have, and they will speak of it to someone else, and before long Sir Thomas' true Brothers of the Order will find and kill you," I said.

"Oh, don't worry, it's almost over, boy, and I promise it will be quick. Well, maybe not. I do so love it when death lasts awhile. But there is one more thing to tell you before I take your life. I want to tell you about the look of stunned surprise and disbelief on Sir Thomas' face when I killed him at the altar of the Crusaders' Palace in Acre." His eyes bore into me and the wind blew through his hair. His snarl made him look like the devil himself.

"No," I gasped. The breath left my lungs. Though I wished to look away, I could not. Curiously, the world around me appeared to be changing color, the white of the snow becoming a hard, hot red. This could not be.

"Oh yes," Sir Hugh said, laughing gleefully. "Such a pompous donkey, your Sir Thomas, always believing himself to be superior. I watched him send you on your way and knew what he had given you. He was hiding it somewhere in the city, and he wouldn't risk having it fall into the hands of the Saracens. So, as he closed the altar behind you—and what a touching little scene it was, by the way . . . *Beauseant,* indeed," he spat. "When he turned around, he laughed! At me! His Commander and Marshal! He said I was too late, and he laughed again. But his laughter died in his throat when I drove my sword through his guts. He died right there in front of me—"

"NO!" I screamed. "You're lying! The other knights, Sir Basil, Quincy, someone would have stopped you! You liar!"

"Feh! Sir Basil and his fat pig of a squire were already dying in the courtyard by then. They're either dead or rotting in one of the Saladin's prisons. No one saw me. I followed you through the tunnel. But I lost you in the countryside. Didn't matter. I knew you had to be heading for Tyre, that Thomas would send you to the Commandery there. It was almost too easy."

"You're a liar!" I screamed, rage rising in my gut. I tried to stand but could not. So help me, I would kill him.

"Enough of this." He smirked. He lifted his sword to shoulder height and came forward, drawing back for a mighty swing, a killing blow.

Just as Sir Hugh came at me, the world slowed down. My eyes opened wide and Sir Hugh advanced in slow motion. One step, then two, then a third. He swung from the shoulder, and his blade whistled, louder than even the sound of the wind.

I lurched to the side and scooped up Sir Thomas' sword in my hands. Rising to my feet, I caught his blow with my sword. The power of it nearly lifted me into the air, but Sir Thomas' blade held. Before he could strike again, I countered, managing to slash his tunic. I don't know where I found the strength, but our steel danced, back and forth, each thrust and parry sending sparks jouncing into the winter wind. As we circled and tested each other, I thought I spied the smallest sense of alarm on Sir Hugh's face. He had expected to dispatch me quickly. Yet I was still standing. Bleeding and growing weaker by the moment, but refusing to give up. I stared down at the satchel, lying on the ground between us, nearly covered in the snow. The Grail remained silent.

My back was to Maryam and Robard. They had been shouting out encouragement, whereas the knights remained silent. But their voices sounded far away, and my concentration remained fixed on Sir Hugh, who charged at me again, his sword swirling back and forth like a whirlwind.

My eyes were still clouded with red rage as he surged toward me, and strange sounds overwhelmed me. Off in the far distance, I thought I heard a familiar bark, but over it all finally it came: the low faint humming sound of the Grail.

For a moment, I believed myself too weak to raise my sword in defense. Sir Hugh had won and this would be my end. But the soft, musical sound grew louder, and as Sir Hugh crossed the ground between us, whether by accident or miracle, he tripped over the satchel. He staggered toward me, glancing down at his feet momentarily. He tried to halt his fall forward but it was too late. His momentum carried him toward me, eyes wide with shock, and with my last bit of strength I thrust forward with Sir Thomas' sword, stabbing Sir Hugh through the ribs.

With a defiant cry of "Beauseant!" I drove my sword deeper into his flesh, and as I did so, for a moment I felt the presence of Sir Thomas, and Quincy, Sir Basil and the abbot and Brother Rupert and the other monks there with me. And my hands became their hands as I pushed with all my might. It felt as if they stood beside me, helping me deliver the world from a great evil. With a groan, I pulled the sword free.

Sir Hugh dropped his blade to the ground. His eyes fell to the seeping wound in his chest. Blood ran from his mouth, and he staggered past me. His horse, standing behind us, pranced out of the way, skittish and spooked at the sight and smell of blood. Confused, Sir Hugh reached down and grasped the satchel in his hands. He staggered backward, holding it as if it were as fragile as a bird's egg.

"No," he said wearily. "Not like this . . . No . . . You *filthy* squire . . . I . . ." He looked at me and his head shook. He shouted at his assembled knights. "Kill them . . . Don't let them get . . . He has it . . . the Grail. . . . Kill them."

I moved toward him and he swung his head up at me, watching me advance.

"No," he said as he staggered backward. "No, not by you. I . . . will . . . not . . . be . . ." Sir Hugh collapsed, falling to the ground right on the edge of the promontory. Then to my horror he began sliding over the side.

And he was taking the Grail with him.

34

No!" I shouted. Everyone remained still. Sir Hugh's momentum built and I doubted I could reach him in time. From somewhere came the strength for me to take three giant steps toward his falling body, and I leapt through the air, landing hard on the ground, grabbing the satchel by its broken strap. Sir Hugh's hands still held firmly to the leather case, and I found myself wondering if it was impossible to kill this man. Then my arm jerked forward and I felt his weight pulling me over with him. I dug and clawed at the ground with my boots, trying to find a toehold, but the wet snow gave me little purchase.

Straining and groaning with the effort, I slid slowly forward, feeling I would surely fall off the cliff with him unless someone intervened. I could hear shouts and noise behind me, but I was now head and chest over the side of the ridge looking down at Sir Hugh hanging there, staring up at me. His eyes were nearly closed in death, the front of his tunic soaked red with blood, but he still spat out the word "Squire . . ."

He lost his grip. His eyes flew open, and for a moment he seemed to hang suspended in the air. With a howl of agony and desperation he fell from the promontory to disappear with a splash into the river far below.

Lying there panting and groaning with the effort, I pushed myself back from the edge of the ridge and staggered to my feet, holding the battered satchel in my hands.

Everyone was stunned. But Robard and Maryam recovered first and took action. Even with his hands bound behind him, Robard lashed out at the knight next to him. Smartly, he kicked the horse in the flank and it reared. The knight fought for control while Robard rolled backward off his own horse. He landed on his feet, shouting loudly and nudging his horse in the flank with his shoulder, sending it scurrying across the circle directly into the path of two other knights.

Maryam gave her ululating war cry, and it added to the noise and confusion. She jumped from her horse and darted beneath it, coming up on the other side and spooking the steed next to her. But it was too little too late. We were outnumbered, Robard and Maryam had no weapons and I feared I would bleed to death shortly. The entire front of my tunic was dark with blood, and my left arm throbbed in pain from the cut I had received.

One of the knights lowered his lance and spurred his horse toward me. It would take only a moment for him to cross the few paces between us. I stood stock-still, unable to raise either arm in my defense. My vision was fading and the world collapsed around me.

As the knight closed in, I focused only on the point of his lance. A horrible way to die, I thought, struck down by a brother of the Order. My last thought was to apologize for failing to protect the Grail as Sir Thomas had wished. But at least Sir Hugh was dead. No matter what happened, he would never be the one to possess the Grail. I hoped it would make Sir Thomas happy.

As death rode down on me, I stood as straight as my wounds would allow, determined to die on my feet. Maryam was shouting at me, but soon it would all be over. I could finally rest.

Then the steel weapon suddenly disappeared, and I looked up in confusion as the knight tumbled backward off his horse. The next thing I knew he was lying on the ground, a crossbow bolt protruding from his chest. What? Some last instinct of survival commanded me to lurch away from the path of the charging horse, and though I jumped aside, the giant animal still collided with me and spun me to the ground.

There was shouting. I heard "Drop your weapons" and suddenly a furry golden flash was over me. It was Angel. She took an instant to bark at me, and I tried to rise up but was too sore and weak. She licked my face, then sniffed at the satchel clutched in my hand, finally sitting on it, as if it were her duty to protect the Grail now.

A shadow fell across the ground in front of me. Someone knelt, placing a hand upon my shoulder. A voice spoke and it sounded familiar. I glanced up thinking for a moment God was playing tricks on me again. For here knelt Sir Thomas, and behind him were several mounted Knights Templar. All of them were pointing crossbows at the knights who had just tried to kill us.

With my last ounce of strength I raised my hand and pointed at Robard and Maryam and said, "Please don't harm those two," and then I fell into a world of blinding white light.

35

T he murmur of voices pulled me to consciousness. I lay on my back and could feel the warmth of a fire. When I opened my eyes, my head was turned to the side and Angel's face was perched perhaps two inches from my own. Her tongue lashed out and licked my nose.

I wanted to roll over and sit up, but the pain of my wounds prevented it. I lay on a pallet next to a large campfire beneath a cloudy sky. It was cold but the fire cut the chill. My shoulder and arm were wrapped in bandages. A priest sat on a cut section of log to my right, near the fire. He smiled and I nodded in return. Maryam and Robard stood on the far side of the fire, a few yards away. Robard leaned on his still-strung bow, Maryam next to him, looking at me with grave concern. She held the satchel in her hand and nodded, indicating it was safe.

Sir Thomas sat on a log next to my left. My heart raced, then dropped to my stomach, for as I studied the man, I realized it wasn't Sir Thomas after all. This knight's hair was a slightly lighter shade, and there was no distinctive scar along his face. His beard was not as thick, and he looked smaller.

"Who . . ." I let my words trail off, mystified.

"You must be Tristan," he said.

"Excuse me, sire——"

"I know. You must be very confused. And in pain. We reached you just in time," he said, gesturing toward my wounded arms. "All thanks to your furry friend there," he said, pointing to Angel. "She found us on our way here, and I can't explain why, but we felt compelled to follow her at a gallop. It was almost as if she were looking for us." He reached over to scratch at Angel's ears. "Your wounds are serious, but we managed to stop the bleeding. How do you feel?" he asked.

"I'm fine. Really. Just flesh wounds," I answered.

He chuckled, and my heart sank again, for his laugh was nearly identical to Sir Thomas'.

"I beg your pardon again, sire, but who——"

"My name is Charles Leux. Thomas is . . . was . . . my younger brother," he said. Now it made sense. His appearance was so similar to Sir Thomas that it made me uncomfortable.

"I'm sorry, sire," I said. "He . . . Sir Thomas . . . Before he died . . . Sir Hugh said he killed him. By the way, Sir Hugh *is* dead, isn't he?"

Charles smiled. "Yes, he's dead, but we have yet to find his body. No one could survive such a fall, though. And I understand you ran him through with a very large sword. As for my brother, well, he may have died doing his duty as a Templar, but I assure you, Tristan, Sir Hugh did *not* kill him."

"How . . . do you know?" I asked.

"I have faith. Sir Hugh is . . . was . . . a coward who preyed on the weak. He would never face Thomas in a fair fight, not even

231

if my brother had lost both his arms." He dropped his head and murmured a brief prayer under his breath. "If my brother is dead, it was not by Hugh's hand. He died fighting, on his feet, like the warrior he was."

None of Sir Charles' words were comforting.

He was silent a moment, then coughed nervously. "I assume you have come here with the Holy Cup of the Savior?" He paused, waiting for me to tell him where it was. "Do you have it with you? Is it safe?"

Something Sir Thomas said in Acre came rushing back. When he had given me the Grail in the Knights Hall, he had said to trust no one. The quest to find and possess the Grail "had turned even my brothers of the Order into glory-crazed hounds."

My expression changed. And Charles noticed immediately.

"You have many questions, I'm sure—" he said, and he reached inside his tunic.

"Robard!" I shouted out in warning.

As always Robard had an arrow nocked and his bow drawn in less than a second and the shaft pointed right at Charles' chest.

"Sire," Robard said quietly, "I must humbly request that you very slowly and gently remove your hand from inside your tunic, lest I be forced to pin it to your chest."

Sir Charles froze for a moment, then smiled. "I see Thomas has trained you magnificently. Of course, you are quite correct not to trust me. Splendid, in fact. But I assure you, I mean you no harm, and what I have here will explain everything. May I remove it? Will you instruct your friend the archer to hold?"

"Slowly. Please remove it very slowly," I said. I was too weak to fight, but felt immense comfort knowing Robard was there to protect me.

Sir Charles removed his hand from his tunic, and in it he held a thick letter. When he held it out, I recognized Sir Thomas' seal, and it looked like a letter Sir Thomas had given me—all those months ago—in Acre. He had commanded I give it to a King's Guard named Gaston. Gaston was to carry the letter back to London to the Master of the Order. At the time, I merely thought the letter was some sort of routine business.

"This is for you," Sir Charles said.

 stared dumbfounded at the letter. Did I now hold Sir Thomas' last words to me in my hand? Sir Charles smiled, and my heart cleaved, for his smile, like his laugh, was so similar to his brother's.

"What is this?" I asked.

"It's something Thomas wanted you to read. Why don't you open it and see for yourself."

"But Sir Thomas told me this letter was for the Master of the Order," I said.

"At your service," said Sir Charles, waving his hand in a small circle and bowing his head slightly.

"You . . . are . . . the Master of the Order?" I stammered.

"Unless my brothers have seen fit to vote me out of office since I left the London Commandery, then yes. I am the Master. Thomas sent the letter with Gaston, who is also a brother of the Order, serving undercover in the King's Guards. One can never be too careful. Monarchs are not always trustworthy, as I'm sure you've learned. So we sometimes keep an eye on them from the inside. Gaston brought the letter to me, as instructed. It was sealed by Thomas' ring, not the Order seal. As we agreed before he left to claim you from St. Alban's, when he sent me a letter sealed with his ring, it was a signal. He was sending you back to England and this letter should be held for you alone. Luckily you didn't die along the way. If you read it, it will answer many of your questions, I'm sure," he said.

With quaking hands I broke the wax seal and spread open the parchment. To my shock and absolute surprise, a small piece of blue cloth tumbled onto my lap that I recognized immediately. It was the missing corner torn from the blanket that had wrapped me as a babe, when I had been left on the steps of St. Alban's.

I stared at Sir Charles in wonderment and he nodded at the parchment. "Just read it. Trust me, lad," he said. I nodded at Robard and he lowered his bow, but being Robard, he kept the arrow nocked.

Looking again at the parchment, I found it covered in Sir Thomas' neat, precise handwriting:

Dear Tristan,

Time is short. I fear with Richard and his main force leaving Acre that we are exposed and weak should the Saladin return. In the days ahead there may be a duty for you to perform, and if I do not survive, I do not wish you to go on through life without the answers you deserve.

Remember our first night in Dover? When I introduced you to King Richard? Remember his shocked expression at meeting you? It's because you are the spitting image of your father. And Richard's father and yours are one and the same.

Your father was Henry II, the former King of England. Your mother was a fine woman, deeply loved by your father. Her name was Rosamund Clifford, and I regret to inform you she no longer lives.

Charles and I served King Henry in his personal guard. When you were born, he and Rosamund knew Eleanor would not rest until she rooted out and destroyed all of Henry's heirs except her own children. Hiding you was the best option. Better you be raised an orphan than murdered in your sleep by Hugh or one of Eleanor's other minions.

Understand, Tristan, this happened through no fault of your own. Your father was in anguish at the thought of taking you from Rosamund, and in truth I believe she died of a broken heart because of it. But they also knew that unless your existence was kept secret, you would never be safe.

Your abbot, Father Geoffrey, was a loyal servant to Henry before he took his vows. It was Charles and I who left you on the abbey steps that night. The abbot was told to make sure you always kept your blue blanket, and I kept this section of it for when the day came that I would be able to prove to you who you are.

Now I fear I will not leave this place, but I will be sure that you at least are freed from Acre. You deserve your chance at life. You have claim to land and title if you choose it. Charles and the Order will support you in whatever you decide.

As for Charles, you can trust him with your life, as you trusted me. He is Master of our Order and Sir Hugh is deathly afraid of him. He will protect you and help you in any way he can. This we promised your father, a great man, a great king, and a father who loved his son.

Go in peace, Tristan. Know you were brought into the world in the full embrace of love. No Knight of the Temple has ever had a finer squire.

Beauseant,
Sir Thomas Leux,

Order of the Poor Fellow Soldiers of Christ and King Solomon's Temple

My hands shook as I stared at Sir Charles.

"May I?" he asked, holding his hand out for the parchment.

I numbly handed it to him and he quickly read it, a smile coming to his face. When he finished, he folded it back up and returned it to me. "So like my brother," he said, smiling as if remembering some pleasant memory.

"How did . . . When did . . . ," I stammered, unable to get the words out.

"We watched over you, Tristan. As you grew, we sent many travelers to St. Alban's to report back to us. You didn't know it and rarely did the abbot. It was the best way. Before he left London for Outremer, Thomas and I talked. He felt it was time to bring you under our protection, to train you, support you and one day perhaps welcome you into the Order as a brother. Yet we had to be cautious, and perhaps Thomas revealed himself too readily by taking an interest in you. Sir Hugh caught on and nearly foiled us."

"But why did Sir Thomas give me the Grail? After making me his squire, shouldn't I have remained with him?" I wondered.

"Perhaps. But the fact that you are here more than answers why he chose you. He chose wisely. At first I argued with him. I was against taking you to Outremer, but we finally agreed, on one condition," he said.

"Which was?"

"He agreed to send you back if it became too dangerous. He would make arrangements to send me this letter, marked with his seal, with the scrap of blanket enclosed. When I received it, I was to keep it until you either returned here or he sent you away. Thomas knew that once King Richard decided not to reinforce Acre, the city could be lost. So he made his preparations, but perhaps the Saracens arrived before he was ready. I think he sent you with the Grail not only because it needed to be saved but because it also gave you a purpose. You were his most loyal servant. He knew you would finish this or die in the attempt. And again, I say he chose wisely."

I was overwhelmed. "I still don't understand, sire. Why me? He could have chosen anyone."

Sir Charles smiled and looked up at the sky. "Let's just say this: Thomas and I loyally served your father. He was a great man. And he commanded us to keep you safe, no matter the cost. As you followed the last order of your knight, we did the same, as the King instructed. When Thomas learned what a fine young man you'd become, he wanted you to have a chance at a good life. That is why he chose you."

I motioned for Maryam to bring me the satchel, and when she handed it to me, I removed the wadded-up blue blanket. Spreading it out before the fire, I held up the piece of cloth Sir Thomas had secreted in the letter. It was a perfect match.

"Sire, this is all . . . I cannot . . . My father was King Henry?"
I stammered.

"Indeed he was, lad. My brother and I guarded your mother,
Rosamund, while you were born. He was torn. He was married
to Eleanor for politics alone. It was a loveless marriage, but at
least it brought temporary peace to two kingdoms. Such is the way
of kings and monarchs. Eleanor returned to France whenever she
could, and your father spent a great deal of time alone. But when he
found Rosamund, he was happy. She was your father's true love."

"What happened to her?" I asked. "Sir Thomas' letter says
she's gone?"

"Yes, lad, I'm sorry to say that not long after you were born,
she caught a fever and passed. I'm sorry you will not have a chance
to know her. She was a fine woman."

The priest who had been sitting there the whole time began to
pray. Maryam had returned to Robard's side, and their faces were
full of questions as they struggled to hear what was going on.

"So what am I to do?" I asked.

"Well, lad, we can discuss it later, but first I think we should
make sure the Grail is safe."

"Yes, sire," I interrupted. "I still have it." I reached inside the
satchel and pulled up the secret bottom, removing the Grail still
wrapped in its white linen covering. Very carefully, I handed it to
Sir Charles, and when I did so, an enormous weight lifted from
my spirit.

"Sir Charles . . . there is something I must tell you . . . ," I said.
"I've been inside Rosslyn. Sir Thomas instructed me to deliver the
Grail to Father William at the Holy Redeemer Church, and I'm
afraid I was too late. Father William is—"

"Father William is sitting right next to you," he said, smiling.

I stared at the priest in shock, not understanding.

"But how? Who—" I was completely confused.

"At your service, Tristan," said the priest from his place beside the fire.

"When Thomas sent me the letter for you from Acre, it was also a signal," Sir Charles said. "I think he knew Richard's foolish plan to leave Acre without reinforcements would mean another attack by the Saracens. He had a dual duty, to keep both you and the Grail safe. When Gaston arrived with the letter, I knew it was also his signal that he would be sending you out with the Grail. I don't think he ever intended for you to do it alone, and I am sure he regretted not being able to send help with you." He paused a moment, letting the words sink in. I believed him. Right after I had given the letter to Gaston, the Saracens had arrived. Sir Thomas had had no choice but to have me escape with the Grail. Now I understood why he had chosen me. I glanced at Maryam and Robard.

"It is all right, sire," I said. "I managed to find help on my own." Sir Charles followed my gaze and beamed at the two of them.

"So it would seem," he said.

"We knew there were brothers inside the order who would kill to possess it. Thomas couldn't be sure that his attempt to have you carry it out and bring it here wouldn't be uncovered. We needed a plan in case anyone discovered your destination or followed you. Like that scoundrel Sir Hugh. So, many weeks ago, we replaced Father William here with a brother from the Order—who sadly gave his life to protect the Grail."

"What is going to happen to the Grail now?" I asked.

"It will be safeguarded forever," Father William said. "Within our small circle of guardians we have plans to build a great cathedral here. And inside that house of the Lord will be—"

"Forgive me for interrupting, Father William," I said. "I'm sure you'll find someplace safe for it, but please don't tell me. I really have no desire to know."

Three Days Later

y wounds healed quickly, and for the next two days we camped near Rosslyn with Sir Charles and his knights. Meals were cooked and stories were told and songs were sung by the fire. We relayed to Sir Charles our exploits along the way, and he became quite fond of Robard and Maryam.

With Sir Charles' blessing, Father William disappeared with the Grail, and I was glad it was now someone else's responsibility. The handful of knights who had assisted Sir Hugh were nowhere in sight, and I thought it best not to wonder what punishment Sir Charles had seen fit to offer them.

One of Sir Charles' sergeantos had tended to my wounds, and after three days' worth of food and rest, I felt ready to leave. The only question was, where would I go? St. Alban's was gone. Sherwood was Robard's home, and I had no idea what Maryam planned to do. She was far from Outremer, but I was certain, given her service in our cause, that Sir Charles would find her passage back if she desired. Whether she wished to return there was the question.

The three of us strolled through the village streets of Rosslyn, Angel at our side. We paused outside the church, and I wondered if

Father William was somewhere inside, finding a secret hiding place for the Holy Grail until his mighty cathedral could be built. For a moment I thought about how, long after my bones had turned to dust, the Grail would still be here, hidden safely away from those who might attempt to use its wonders for ill purposes.

"What are you going to do, your highness?" Robard asked me.

"Stop calling me that! I'm not a highness!" I replied, only slightly annoyed. Ever since we had learned my true identity, Robard had delighted in teasing me about it.

"Seriously, Tristan, what are your plans?" Maryam asked. "You English and your laws are confusing, but what will you do? Sir Charles says you have claims to land—"

"I don't want it," I interrupted her. "You've met Eleanor and Sir Hugh? And I've met Richard, and I could do without the lot of them. I don't care about land or title, and I certainly will make no claim to the throne. Not even with the backing of the Order. It's all too much. Far too much. From Outremer, I carried the weight of the Grail. I have no desire to carry anything so heavy again. I have a different plan in mind," I said.

"Really?" Robard asked, snickering again.

"Yes, Robard, a real genuine plan. Thanks for asking. What are you two going to do?"

When Robard and Maryam's eyes met, they danced with joy. She was not going back to Outremer, at least not now, and maybe not ever.

"We're going to return to Sherwood for a while," Robard said. "Maryam has never seen the forest in the spring and summer. I want to show her the meadows and the fields. I want her to see the chestnuts and the sycamores come to bud. There are many things I want her to know." Maryam smiled at him and gently slipped her hand into his.

"And what of the Shire Reeve?" I asked.

"What of him? I think he's learned his lesson. I doubt he'll soon bother the good folk of Sherwood again," Robard said assuredly. I smiled and nodded, though I did not share Robard's confidence. I would not ruin Robard's high spirits, but the Shire Reeve of Nottingham did not strike me as someone who would give up so easily.

"But enough about us, Tristan. What is this plan you have?" Maryam asked eagerly.

When I told them, they smiled and clapped me on the back.

"Come," I said. "Let's find Sir Charles and I'll tell him what I've decided. He's at his tent outside the gate."

We were a few strides down the street when I realized Angel was not at her usual place, loping along beside us. Looking back, I saw that she sat on her haunches in front of the church.

"Come, Angel!" I called to her. But she didn't move.

"Is she sick?" Maryam asked, concerned. "She always comes when you call her."

"I don't know. Angel, come!" I called again. Yet she remained where she was. The three of us strode down to the church steps and studied her. She stared up at us, her brown intelligent eyes shining in the morning light.

"Come on, girl," I said. "It's time to go."

Angel whined, then stood and pushed her head against my hand. I rubbed her head and ears, and she moved to Robard and he did the same. When she reached Maryam, she flopped onto her back and Maryam rubbed her belly vigorously.

"Angel," I said. "Stop this. It's time to go."

She barked once, then darted away around the corner of the church, heading down the alley between it and the adjacent building.

"What in the world . . . ," I said, and we all trotted after her. But when we reached the corner and peered down the alley, she was gone.

"Where is she?" Maryam spoke, her voice shaking as if she might cry.

I thought back to how I had found her, lounging in the sun in the alley in Tyre, near the place where I had hidden the Grail. How she had kept it safe and delivered it to me when I returned for it. On our entire journey she had guided us, barking out warnings, sniffing the air, sounding the alarm whenever danger was near. But always, she safeguarded the Grail. Maybe her journey was over as well. Maybe God wanted her here in Rosslyn, keeping the Grail safe.

"I think . . . ," I said.

"What?" Maryam said, tears forming in her eyes.

"Perhaps her duty is here," I said.

"No . . . ," Maryam said.

But I felt it was true. Where the Grail was, Angel would stay. She was its guardian, not ours. We stared at the empty alleyway for a few more moments, then turned and left for the Templar camp.

It was time for new beginnings.

obard and Maryam were mounted up. In his generosity, Sir Charles had given them two fresh steeds and a packhorse with enough supplies to last long enough for their journey back to Sherwood. He also told Robard that when he reached the nearest commandery, he would send a letter to William Wendenal explaining how Robard Hode had done great service to the Order, and asking him for forgiveness of all crimes and transgressions.

"I can't promise it will do any good," Sir Charles said, "but I am not without some influence with Prince John, and I will make every effort to see to it that you and your folk are not bothered by this troublesome Shire Reeve."

"Thank you, Sir Charles," Robard said, giving him a small salute. Sir Charles stepped away, giving me privacy while I said goodbye to my friends.

"Take care, Tristan," Robard said, extending his hand. I shook it firmly.

"And you as well, Robard. You have a chance to do something

good in Sherwood, to help the poor and the weak. If this Shire Reeve . . . well . . . just promise me you'll always fight with honor," I said.

"I promise," he said, smiling. Maryam jumped down from her horse to give me one last hug good-bye.

"You be careful. We won't be there to save you from your outrageous plans anymore," she said.

"I know. I'll be careful, I promise. And try to keep Robard out of trouble, will you?" She laughed and mounted her horse again.

"What trouble?" Robard asked indignantly. "Me? Trouble? I hardly think so! You've been nothing but a trial since I rescued you from those bandits in the Holy Land. Why does everyone always think I'm the one who will get into trouble?"

"And one more thing: please watch over Tuck. He's the only family I have left—well, at least family that's not trying to kill me. And I feel like he's found a new home in Sherwood. Please try to make him understand I'll return to see him someday."

Maryam nodded her assent. And Robard stared at me and smiled.

"What?" I asked.

"I heard it," he said.

"Heard what?" I ask.

"Your vase. The Grail. On the cliff at Montségur, when I was falling, I heard it. A soft musical hum. It was the strangest thing. As I was hurtling to my death, I felt no fear, only comfort. I knew, I don't understand how, but I *knew* you would catch me," he explained.

"Perhaps you are more righteous than you claim, archer," I said smiling.

"Wouldn't it be nice to think so," he said softly.

We were silent for a moment, not wanting our time together to end. Then they reined their horses around and headed home. I watched them ride until they disappeared from sight.

Sir Charles was suddenly there beside me. "Are you ready, lad?" he asked, his voice reminding me so much of Sir Thomas that it made my heart ache.

"Yes, sire, I am ready." We mounted our horses, Sir Charles taking Sir Hugh's fine stallion and myself happy to be sitting atop Charlemagne once again.

"Are you sure you wouldn't like a different horse?" he asked.

"I'm quite sure, sire," I said.

We left Rosslyn, turning southeast toward the coast. My new life would start once we reached Dover.

Two weeks later inside the chapel of the Dover Commandery, I knelt before Sir Charles, Master of the Order of the Knights Templar. With Sir Thomas' battle sword, he touched me on the shoulder. I had asked Sir Charles for membership in the Order as a knight. Since he knew I was of noble birth, he agreed to sponsor me. He also granted my request for the ceremony to be held in Dover. During our ride back from Scotland and in the past few days here, he had instructed me on all the rules and laws a Templar Knight was required to obey. With his blessing, I knelt before him.

I looked up at the tapestries lining the chapel walls, each of them showing moments of our history as Templar Knights. Studying them, I felt a part of something in a way I never had before. We were not a perfect order, but perfection was not a human trait. Yet men like Sir Thomas and Sir Charles understood that honor, duty and sacrifice were more than just words. Now I would join them in spirit and make a commitment to live my life as they lived theirs, bound by a promise of service to those less fortunate, to defend the weak and the defenseless. The thought of it humbled me beyond all measure.

"In the name of the Father, Son and Holy Ghost, I dub thee Sir Tristan, Brother Knight of the Poor Fellow Soldiers of Christ and King Solomon's Temple, with all the rights and privileges such rank accords."

The other brothers in attendance cheered, and when I stood, Sir Charles handed me Sir Thomas' sword, which I sheathed at my belt. Someday, I would send word to Little John that I needed a new short sword for when I selected a squire. Carrying the big sword felt right now.

"You're a Brother Knight, Tristan. How does it feel?" Sir Charles asked me.

"It feels wonderful, sire," I said, looking down at my bright white tunic with the red cross emblazoned across my chest.

"Have you thought about where you would like to be posted?" he asked.

"Yes, sire. I have. With your permission, I wish to be assigned to a commandery in the south of France."

"Really? So far from England?" he asked, his eyebrows arching up. I thought of that day in France, when Celia and I had stood high atop the walls of Montségur. I saw the wind whip her hair around her face and the impossibly blue color of her eyes. Thinking of her again made me smile.

"Yes, sire. I have business there," I said. "Unfinished business."

GODSTOW NUNNERY,
OXFORDSHIRE, ENGLAND
ONE WEEK LATER
JANUARY 1192

Epilogue

he nunnery appeared deserted as I rode through the main gate, but there was no doubt I had already been watched for some time. It was a beautiful winter morning, spring would be here soon, and it would be welcome. Last evening I had spent a great deal of time polishing my chain mail and sword, and they glinted in the warm sunlight. In Dover, I had been newly outfitted with boots and mail, and my white tunic had remained relatively mud-free on my morning ride.

I dismounted and tied Charlemagne to a nearby hitching post. The old plow horse stamped his foot at the grass beneath the light dusting of snow as I waited patiently in the courtyard.

Finally the main door opened and an elderly nun made her way down the steps, approaching me cautiously.

"Greetings to you, traveler," she said meekly.

"Thank you, Sister. My name is Tris . . . Sir Tristan"—I still was getting used to the sound of it—"of the Knights Templar and I wonder if you could help me." When I told her what I wanted, she smiled and, pulling her cloak up tightly around her, led me behind the nunnery to a small gated cemetery. She pointed out a small stone inside the graveyard and left me there alone.

I knelt before her marker, the final resting place of my mother, Rosamund Clifford.

Looking up at the sky, I closed my eyes, letting the warm sun strike my face, and for a moment I imagined the sunlight was her touch embracing me. I prayed silently, asking God to grant her peace had he not already done so. I crossed myself and stood. Then I removed Sir Thomas' Templar ring from my cloak and placed it upon the stone marker. I did not think the nuns would accept it from me if I offered it to them directly. But they would find it when I left, and such a ring when sold would feed the nunnery for many months. I thought it would make Sir Thomas happy. Besides, I now had my own Templar ring to wear.

Looking down at the marker one last time, I said good-bye to my mother. I left the cemetery, closing the gate behind me, and returned to the courtyard where Charlemagne waited patiently for me. Jumping into the saddle, I gave a small salute to the nuns I knew were watching from the windows.

Then I turned the gentle plow horse toward the gate, and together we rode off into the cool, fine morning.

†HE END